So Far *from* Story Street

So Far *from* Story Street

A Novel

J. P. LaVallee

authorHOUSE®

AuthorHouse™
1663 Liberty Drive
Bloomington, IN 47403
www.authorhouse.com
Phone: 1-800-839-8640

Published by AuthorHouse   01/24/2013

ISBN: 978-1-4817-0446-5 (sc)
ISBN: 978-1-4817-0445-8 (hc)
ISBN: 978-1-4817-0447-2 (e)

Library of Congress Control Number: 2013900212

Table of Contents

Dedication

This book is dedicated to my great uncle, Arthur G. LaVallee, upon whose life this story is based.

I hope that his young spirit has been evoked in the telling of his tale; it lives in me.

—J.P. LaVallee

J. P. LaVallee

In Flanders Fields

In Flanders fields the poppies blow
Between the crosses, row on row,
That mark our place; and in the sky
The larks, still bravely singing, fly
Scarce heard amid the guns below.

We are the Dead. Short days ago
We lived, felt dawn, saw sunset glow,
Loved and were loved, and now we lie,
In Flanders fields.

Take up our quarrel with the foe:
To you from failing hands we throw
The torch; be yours to hold it high.
If ye break faith with us who die
We shall not sleep, though poppies grow
In Flanders fields.

—John McCrae, May 3, 1915

Chapter One

The End of a Gilded Age

Already, the flames were engulfing a great section of the city, beginning with the area of Boston Street, before enough had realized what was going on. Black clouds rose up, and the great fire was rapidly nearing our South Salem neighborhood. I ran downstairs to find my father and brother, and together we started hosing down the roof of the house and my grandfather's Barber Shop on Story Street, but this was to no avail; we knew that the encroaching blaze would soon sweep across our block, for we felt a heavy heat in the air. It was four in the morning. The Audets, across the street, started clearing out all of the merchandise from the shelves of their general store, and packing it all into boxes and then packing the boxes into their small wagon. We were all soon thereafter given orders from the authorities to 'evacuate to higher ground' at Forest River Park.

My brother and I both darted inside our rooms in the three-story house that my grandfather had built in order to gather our most cherished belongings. I immediately went for my photo albums and scrapbooks, grabbing as many as I could. Pete went for his prized train collection, stuffing each engine and boxcar into a large laundry sack. My father's voice then sounded, *Joseph! René! Valère! Pete! Venez, vite!* He had managed to gather up some of his *bricolage* tools and to find my mother and sister. We were greeted by a horse and carriage filled with other neighbors heading southeast to the public park. We rode along Lafayette Street, past St. Joseph's, the Saltonstall School, the Credit Union and Loring Square, until we reached the grounds at Forest River Park. We watched vermillion flames and blackness spread through South Salem down to the mills at Congress Street, then on through the Waterfront district, near Pickering Wharf, and my heart pounded.

The devastation left almost all of my friends and family members homeless. I later viewed this apocalyptic event as my induction into adulthood, for we celebrated my eighteenth birthday at the Forest River Park refuge, among the tents and makeshift beds, among many friends and neighbors who also managed to escape the flames. The Audets, our neighborhood grocers, made the occasion even more special by donating a bag of penny candy to every child encamped there.

Three days later—in the midst of this time of crisis—some folks there had heard news hailing from the Continent that there had been an assassination in a place called 'Sarajevo'. Someone from a noble family and his wife had been shot by a group of six assassins while traveling in an open-topped automobile. They were there—it was said—to observe military maneuvers in the city and to open a new museum. It seems as if it is all due to something called 'nationalism', which seems to me to be some kind of new *disease* that is making its way around Europe.

* * *

A week after our displacement, we received a load of statistics from the local officials: due to the Great Fire, over 3,500 families lost their homes—that is about 20,000 people in all; and 253 acres were burned along with 1,376 buildings. The damage in dollars has yet to be calculated, but it must be some unfathomable number.

2

A storefront on Rantoul Street in Beverly eventually became our family's new, temporary home, after two weeks of living in the small tents. My siblings—Florida, René, Pete, and Valère—and I helped make the place feel cozier by putting up family *daguerreotypes* on the walls of the two large rooms that we occupied. Meanwhile, even while embers were still smoldering, there was already some rebuilding going on back in South Salem. We all made the daily trip by horse and buggy with other displaced Salemites, along Rantoul Street Bridge over the Salem Sound, to Story Street to pitch in our efforts. Since we had also lost the hub of the wheel of our community, Saint Joseph's Church and Rectory, that's where we began.

Our relatives up on Castle Hill were not troubled at all by the blaze, thank goodness; Uncle François said that the wind changed direction, and although they were ready with hoses to wet down the roofs of their homes and Sainte Anne's church, the flames never traveled that far south.

This demon fire had begun, we learned, with a series of explosions caused by a mixture of stored chemicals that are used to make patent leather on shoes, at the Korn Leather Factory. The explosions went off a little before two in the morning, and then the fire quickly spread down Boston Street and across the city while we were all asleep. Ten thousand people lost their jobs, including my father who worked at the Naumkeag Steam Cotton Company. We had never seen such devastation; most of our city was a ruin, and the sight of it reminded me of the pictures I had seen of Ancient Rome and Pompeii in our Latin textbooks. The only collective thought now was how we were to recreate our beloved neighborhood as soon as possible. We were starting from scratch.

Chapter Two
Préparations

S ummer vacation is now in full swing, and the duties of school are behind me, at least for the next eight weeks. These weeks stretch out like a vast, inviting meadow before me. The final days of June are a festive time in Montaigu and in every other village, town and city, every year. Preparations began today for our celebration of *La Fête de la Bastille,* my favorite holiday. The Day, which turns into a week-long party, is also a time when I have the chance to see my cousins from the south, whom I usually see only twice-a-year. I like the tasks designated for me and my younger brother at this time: Henri and I are charged with organizing the decoration of the barn with the *tricolored* banners, and also the fireworks displays for all of the Pasquiers and our friends. The company of my immediate and extended family is welcome; and I like to work in tandem with my mother and aunts who take care of the cooking. The family banquet is a meal that I look forward to for weeks, and one that me and my large family savor all together on the lengthy picnic table located under the shade of large chestnut tree in the yard beside our long, two-story stucco house. My mother combs the marketplaces of the *commune* to gather what she discerns to be the very finest herbs, vegetables, fruits, meats, cheeses and wines to be consumed. *My* task is to provide an accompaniment to these delights by preparing a feast for the eyes—those bursts of rainbow-colored lights in the sky; so today, Henri and I went off to procure fireworks from the regional distributor's in La Vendée's *préfecture*, La-Roche-sur-Yon. This year, the family's plan was to ride to Challans and to launch them from the nearby Ile de Noirmoutier, accessible only during low tide, when the single road to the island is no longer submerged. We did so two years ago when I was sixteen, and my brother and I agree that the *feux d'artifice* were more spectacular-looking that year. From the mainland, it appeared as if the colors and lights popped up from the great Atlantic itself, and so we think that it would be splendid to repeat such a spectacle in a fortnight. All of my aunts and uncles will be so pleased, and this thought makes me very happy.

La-Roche-sur-Yon is a good thirty-minute horse and buggy ride from Montaigu. The poplar tree-lined dirt roads are best to travel during the late morning hours, when there is the least amount of travelers on them. So, after breakfast, Henri and I harnessed our two favorite mares from the stable, and made our way to the capital, making good time, over the slightly hilly countryside. It was brilliantly sunny day, with only a hint of a cloud in the distance, to the southeast.

The *préfecture* is a bustling place, that is, in comparison with our little village. One can find a central post office, a large market square adjacent to the *Hôtel de Ville*, a police station, a small hospital, and many, many shops. My favorite is the LaGrange's Smoke Shop that houses hundreds of boxes of cigars, bags of tobaccos, and several kinds of pipes, organized on mahogany shelves which cover three of the four walls. Every time I am in town, I stop in and ask the proprietor, Monsieur LaGrange, for any spare cigar boxes that he may have stored away. These are perfect for storing my various collections, which include rocks, shells, *centimes,* and my lucky rabbits' feet. I usually come away with one or two boxes, as well as a small bag of tobacco and some cigarette rolling papers that I share with Henri.

5

A trip to town is also not complete without stopping at the neighboring news kiosk for the weekly *France-Dimanche*. Today there was young vendor who stood next to a sandwich board posting the paper's front page, and who called out loudly, *"Supplément de nouvelles! Supplément! Assassination à Sarajevo!"* From the ruckus the boy was making, Henri and I knew that there was some major calamity somewhere, probably in Paris. But after purchasing the newspaper and reading the headline for ourselves, we found out that a nobleman from Austro-Hungary was killed by a young Serbian terrorist. We learned that Sarajevo is located in a place called Bosnia. Why, we both wondered, did such a faraway event seem to matter so much to the likes of the folks of LaVendée? I supposed that they were trying to sell more papers. We purchased a newspaper for our family, as we usually did, and when we left the scene our thoughts returned to our errand-running.

The next stop was Monsieur Defarge's *Bastille Day Bastion*, a large warehouse which we patronize to supply our family with the fireworks needed for the big day. Today Mr. Defarge, wearing his patriotic blue, white and red work apron, was at the counter himself, extremely busy with several customers. His three sons were in the back, stuffing cardboard boxes with orders, and loading them onto the company wagon for local deliveries. After exchanging greetings with the proprietor, and catching up on family news, Henri and I ordered several rockets, sparklers, Catherine wheels, fiery fountains, and aerial mortars, and loaded everything into our wagon with the help of the Defarge brothers.

We finished our errands, mounted our buggy, and went back home; the only real difference from earlier in the morning, we noticed, was that the small cloud looming in the southeast had grown a little bigger.

Chapter Three

The Aftermath

Roland and his family moved in with friends in Lynn, and I miss him terribly. We have had no way of visiting each other or of talking to each other for many days, which seem like years. I suppose that he is doing as well as can be expected, and that he has found a job at the General Electric plant in South Lynn, like many of the other displaced citizens of Salem. If I know *him*, he is riding a bicycle around the city, and back-and-forth to work on fair weather days.

My father and I make daily trips over to South Salem to help the construction workers rebuild Story Street. Clearing away the debris of the burned structures is the business of each day. It is a massive effort on the part of city workers and denizens of the area, as we are all eager to begin the rebuilding process. My mother, the 'business woman' of our family, has the biggest hand in making the plans for the construction of a multi-family house in our neighborhood a reality, as she is—in a headstrong way—negotiating the cost and choice of building materials with the municipal folks. Our aim is to be able to finish most of the outdoor work by Thanksgiving, before the bitter cold of the mid-winter months grips the region. A grand, coordinated effort on the part of governments to rebuild our city helps a great deal. Even President Wilson wrote: "I am sure I speak for the American people in tendering heartfelt sympathy to you to the stricken people of Salem. Can the federal government be of service to you in the emergency?"

Local newspapers, each day, print new ordinances for the reconstruction of the city put forward by the City Council and the newly-formed Salem Rebuilding Commission—made up of five local men. For example, it was written: "Hereafter all roofs that shall be constructed, altered or repaired shall be covered with slated or other incombustible material, and that the gutter shall be of metal or covered with metal." The first building permit was granted on July 13th to a Mister J. Dube for a permanent building, a two story brick bakery at 16 Leavitt Street. On that day the newly-formed Commission held its first public meeting at Ames Memorial Hall, where many prominent citizens spoke out on the laying-out of streets. And on the next day, the Commission gave a hearing to the Lafayette Street residents—whose properties abutted our neighborhood, who had a live committee made up of five members, including our friend, Mister Poirier. These members called for: "Wires underground or on ornamental poles; trees planted along Lafayette Street; three-deckers prohibited in this district; no stores or shops of Lafayette Street from Harbor Street up; park bounded by Harbor, Lafayette and Washington Streets; no courts or private ways off Lafayette Street." The Commission also ruled that "no wooden structures of any sort" could be built within the burned district. But later it was stated that the wooden house matter was being considered, as the cost of brick far exceeded that of wood; and then a Mr. Sullivan won out his contention for wooden buildings "with a covering of incombustible material". At these meetings and in the air in general we felt, despite some periods of negotiation, a splendid spirit of optimism which carries us over the hard places, with the belief that we will prevail in the future and that a city—far better than the Salem-of-the-past—will rise from these ruins.

I am not able to return to my job at the A. Goos Factory in North Salem, where I drive the company horse and buggy; for it, too, has been devastated by the Fire. Instead, I am now delivering groceries in Beverly for the grocer on Cabot Street. My brothers and sister have also found odd jobs in our adopted town, as we patiently await our return to the neighborhood. The days do not seem to pass quickly enough in this state of *limbo*, as I have a constant yearning to see Roland and my other friends and the familiar faces of Story Street—the Audets, the Blanchettes, the Lesveques, the Moreaus, and the Pelletiers . . . . I am also eager to help out with the rebuilding of our 'Little Canada'.

*   *   *

The Fourth of July was soon upon us, and its festivities were a welcome respite from the work of debris-clearing and rebuilding. There was no cookout on Story Street this year; instead, we all went down to the Willows for some fried clams and to watch the fireworks. René and I went ahead, and then at nightfall we were joined by the rest of our family, and also some neighbors. The best part for me was that, at last, I was able to see Roland, who met us there later in the afternoon.

It was a clear day, but *hot*, so the Willows Park was *the place to be*. We had a grand time eating seafood at Swenbeck's, savoring an ice cream cone from Hobbs' while walking along the pier, and we even took a ride on the flying-horses carousel. The sound of the band instruments playing "By the Beautiful Sea" at the Waterfront filled the air, and a cool breeze blew from the ocean and made the branches of the willow trees sway. Refreshment came in all forms that day.

The fun came to an end all-too-soon, and we were back at work the very next day. Builders were at work on several three-family houses and small apartment buildings that lined Story Street. My mother was right beside them, giving instructions. There was also a lot of progress made on the church and rectory, with the priest and sisters feeling confident that structures would be ready to house school children by summer's end for the start of a new school year. The church had sustained terrible damage in the Fire, including the destruction of the valuable stained glass windows and the sacristy. Now we could see some progress being made on its reconstruction, with the use of white brick, instead of wood. There would be a structure in place for a school, come September.

Chapter Four

Bastille Day

Our town was awash with the colors of the *tricolore*, and I was filled with anticipation for the festivities that would come in just a few hours. In the town center, on the gazebo—the spot where the *bal musette* had been set up last night—a small ensemble of local musicians gathered to play a round of patriotic songs. Even from the distance of our farm—a kilometer away—one could hear the melody of *La Marseillaise* floating through the air on the balmy, summer breezes of the day. And I could hear many-a-neighbor chiming in with the words that are embossed in our brains and hearts: *Allons enfants de la Patrie, le jour de Gloire est arrivéééé* . . . , as they went about their party preparations, even after a full evening of dancing the night before.

The *cloche* in church tower struck twelve o'clock noon, and that signaled the start of the regional parade. Local bands played their hearts out and the many clubs had each created a festive float to show off. Henri and I dressed in blue, white and red, made our way quickly to the *Hôtel de Ville* and headed straight to the balloon man, Monsieur LeClerc—as we did every year—to help him with sales. He gave us each a money apron, and we walked up and down the *Rue Saint Joseph* shouting *"Ballons, 50 centimes!"* I especially loved looking at the many different costumes and uniforms, and comparing the quality and creativity of floats, one to the other, as I sold balloons to the parents of small children. This year, the most majestic float was the model of the Bastille, painted a bronze color, perched on a cart covered with a platform, and surrounded by seven people dressed as the "prisoners". At the parade's end, Monsieur LeClerc gave Henri and me a generous payment of five francs, plus a free balloon for our efforts; and, as usual, we spent this sum on sweets at the central *pâtisserie*.

The dispersal of the spectators, after the sound of the footsteps of the final marchers faded, meant that it was time to return home for the continuation of the day-long party, the midday feast. Our entire family, immediate and extended, now gathered all together for *la fête*. The picnic table, long and wooden, was covered with a red linen cloth, used expressly for this day of the year for the assembled *compagnie*. *Le grand déjeuner*—a selection of the most delectable, and favorite dishes—covered the cloth, along with three bouquets of wildflowers and sixteen table settings. My cousins soon arrived from La Rochelle, bringing along with them the tastiest desserts: lemon meringue and strawberry chiffon pies, butter cream cakes, and *petits gâteaux*. For the first time, we had also invited some neighbors from down the road, as this feast was usually reserved for family members only. They brought along with them some regional wines from their family cellars, which delighted my parents.

A round of croquet to play with whoever was game, before the start of the meal, typically took place. Our neighbors—Michel and David who were twins, and Monique their sister, one year younger, and who attend the local *collège* with me—were happy to take up a mallet with my brother and me. I made sure that I took my turn directly after Monique, so that I would be able to stand next to her. I was glad—for the rest of the day—that our family had made an exception to the 'family only' rule. And it turned out that Monique was brilliant at croquet, and it was she, the only girl among the players, who won the match.

Our afternoon unfolded in a most agreeable way. The eating and drinking *en plein air* lasted for three hours, with little breaks for clearing one dish, and presenting another. The sun shone brilliantly overhead, there was a pleasant breeze, and the birds in our midst seemed to be as filled with patriotic song as we all were. By six o'clock we were all ready for more games, so there was a *football* game, and also later some tennis added to our family tradition which we played at the neighbors' place down the road.

At dusk Henri and I made the announcement that we should all begin to make our way over to the island where we planned to launch our fireworks. A small convoy of buggies was assembled for the forty-five minute ride to the coast. The tide was low, of course, which allowed our passage to the off-shore Ile de Noirmoutier. The four hours allotted us would pass quickly, so we had to stay aware of the time, or else the only road connecting the mainland to the island would be completely submerged, and thus impassable, once the tide came in.

The night sky was full of stars, and once the fireworks display began, promptly at nine o'clock, it glittered even more brightly. After I launched my round of Catherine wheels, I let Henri take over. I looked for Monique and found her sitting under a tree by herself, and so I took a seat next to her. Her cheerful eyes greeted me, and we both smiled at each other. I pulled myself a little closer to her side, and put my arm around her waist, and then I felt a tingle move up my spine.

She said to me: "Are you cold? You're shivering!"

"No, not cold." I said, elongating my smile.

We knew then that a special friendship had begun, and we felt very lucky to know each other. I thought about my rabbit's foot, hanging from my trousers by a small chain, and I grinned. Together, we admired the light show in the sky, as we continued to hold hands. Never have I enjoyed someone's company so much.

The spectacle came to an end much too soon, and we had to make our way off the island quickly. We could see the ocean water approaching; the tide was coming in as fast as a horse can gallop. The salty water was already lapping the roadside when we reached the mainland: we won the race! It had been a most beautiful day.

Chapter Five

The Guns of August

It had been a sultry early August evening, and just now a thick, grey cloud looms overhead, as nightfall approaches. Last night the *appel* rang out from the *Hôtel de Ville* that all young men, able bodied, were to register with the district *légioniers*: it is a call to battle, after so many years of peace in France. Tonight we await our assignment to a fighting unit, and then we will be issued a uniform, some gear, and a train ticket to Paris. And thus, a new, young French *armée* is now being assembled from all corners of the land. Many young Frenchmen, I know, have the echoes of the voices of their ancestors in their ears, and the tune of the patriotic *Marseillaise* is rising up from those spirits, and fills the air: *Aux armes, Citroyens! Formez vos bataillons! Marchons! Marchons!* The pace quickens; the saunter and smile of yesterday have been forgotten.

We dropped everything, Henri and I and many others, and followed the orders imposed upon us. Overnight, we have been placed on a new path, by forces beyond our own control; that is, by the aggression of neighboring Germans who are now pouring in from the east, a river of steel. The word on the streets of Montaigu is that we, the young men, have to be *déployés* as quickly as humanly possible. As far as official intelligences are aware, German infantrymen, now goose-stepping through

Brussels as we take arms, are planning to seize hold of Paris; and the word is that they are now rapidly making their way through the forests of Namur, having easily swept through Belgian capital, all the while singing *"Mein Vaterland, Mein Vaterland!"*

I have always heard my father and grandfather praise *la Patrie,* and I have heard them say that they would lay down their lives for their country as an act of honor. Yet to me, this is a foreign idea. These concepts of *honneur* and *noblesse,* which have been passed down to me through many, many generations—from the time of Gaul, or even beforehand, before the Fall of Troy—have not taken hold in my heart; and yet, it now falls to me and my generation to act on this abstraction. I also now realize that the very same concepts have long been firmly established in the minds of those from neighboring lands, as well. I feel as if suffocated: the pressure to take part in this undertaking is unbearable. Tomorrow I will board the train to Paris, along with Henri and the twins, Michel and David, and with my lucky rabbit's foot in my pocket.

Chapter Six
A Letter from the Marne

Créteil
le 7 septembre, 1914

Chère Maman,

On est—Henri et moi—maintenant dans la ville de Créteil, près de la Marne, de quinze kilomètres de Paris; c'est assez gris ici.

Tu peux être rassurée que nous sommes, pour le moment, protégés par nos camarades, par Papa Joffre, et par les barrières naturelles des tributaires de la Marne—qui séparent nous les français, des boches. Mais l'air est très agité.

Les nouvelles les plus fantasitques—qui viennent de nous arriver—sont que des taxis et des autobus de Paris forment maintenant une sorte de défilé, et ils transportent des hommes armés de toutes régions de la France vers le front. Alors, nous sommes peut-être sauvés. Nous avons déja perdu des milliers de soldats aux fusils des allemands. On n'a pas de choix que d'écouter les mots du Générale qui nous entourent: "Le moment de regarder en arrière est passé; mourrez dans vos pas plutôt que se replier!"

Je prie. J'emploie chaque jour le bouquin de prières que tu m'as donné au départ. La prière préferée d'Henri s'appelle 'la Prière du Matin':

> Au nom du Père, du Fils, et du Sainte Esprit. Mon Dieu, je vous adore comme mon Créateur et mon Souverain Maître. Je vous remercie de tous les biens que j'ai reçus de vous et pour l'âme et pour le corps. Mon Dieu, je crois en vous: fortifiez ma foi. Mon Dieu, j'espère en vous: je ne serai jamais confondu. Mon Dieu, je vous aime de tout le coeur et pour l'amour de vous j'aime mon prochain comme moi-même. Je vous offre, Seigneur, toutes mes pensées, toutes mes paroles, toutes mes actions de ce jour: Faites-moi la grâce de le passer saintement. Ainsi soit-il.

Ces mots nous fortifient.

Tu me manques infiniment. Dis 'bonjour' à Papa et à Monique de ma part, s'il te plaît.

Ton fils,
—Philippe.

*   *   *

Créteil
September 7, 1914

Dear Mom,

We are—Henri and I—in the town of Créteil now, near the Marne, about fifteen kilometers from Paris; it is pretty grey here.

You can be reassured that we are, for the moment, protected by our comrades, by Papa Joffre, and by the natural barriers of the tributaries of the Marne which separate us, the French, from the boches. But the air is very agitated.

The most fantastic news—which just arrived—is that some taxis and buses coming from Paris are forming a kind of parade, and are transporting armed men from all regions of France to the front. So, we will, perhaps, be saved. We have already lost many thousands of soldiers at the guns of the Germans. We have no choice but to listen to the words of the General which surround us: "The time for looking backward has passed. Die in your tracks rather than retreat!"

I am praying. Each morning I use the prayer book that you gave to me upon departure. Henri's favorite prayer is called "The Morning Prayer":

> In the name of the Father, the Son, and the Holy Spirit. My God, I adore you as my Creator and my Sovereign Master. I thank you for all the good things that I have received from you and for my spirit and my body. My God, I believe in you: strengthen my faith. My God, I put my hope in you: I will never be confused. My God, I love you with all my heart, and for the love of you I love the next one as I love myself. I offer to you, Lord, all of my thoughts, all of my words, all of my actions of this day. Provide for me the grace to spend it in a holy way. Amen.

These words fortify us.

I miss you immeasurably. Please say 'hello' to Dad and to Monique from me.

Your son,
—*Philippe.*

19

Chapter Seven

The End of Innocence

A call rang through the streets of Salem at three thirty that mid-June morning, via a bell system from the Salem Militia Headquarters on Essex Street. This meant that I was to report to the Armory along with Roland, and neighbors—Armand and Léonard, and other friends, before the sun rose. We were about to become young soldiers, part of a 'Yankee Division'. We heard that it was our President Wilson who submitted the call for young men to defend the southern United States border from a Mexican aggressor named Pancho Villa. I was to turn twenty years old in a little over a fortnight, and I was aware that my quiet life in the South Salem neighborhood was about to be changed forever.

We, those called to arms, were now under military rule, each hour of the day. Cots were set up in the Armory, and we were ordered to relocate to that address until further notice. Luckily, Roland, Stanis and I got passes to return home for a few hours that evening, when we shared supper and whatever news we had of what was to come.

"Bet we'll have to board a train and head out tomorrow, at the crack of dawn." Roland said.

"You're right . . . Story Street looks different to me today than it did yesterday." I answered. "It's as if I'm looking at it from a distance, and everything seems smaller."

The next day we were held in the Armory for the entire day. I was put on guard duty at the rear door on Brown Street, and I decided to slip out without a pass to return home for the evening. I wanted to see my parents and my brothers and sister, because I had the feeling that I would be taken away from them within the next few days.

Indeed, we were ordered to board a train bound for the mobilization camp in Framingham early the next morning, the first day of summer. We would all have to become used to looking at our watches and forgetting about our dreams. We moved by troop train from the Salem Depot at 8:35, and arrived in Boston a little after "nine hundred hours", and at 9:15 we were ordered to march across the city to South Station, and there we entrained at half past two. The irony was that it was the first day of the solstice, and a lovely, sunny day, a day that usually signals the coming of good times, including cookouts and other family gatherings. But instead, here we were marching further and further away from our personal freedoms. On the other hand, there is a kind of patriotic euphoria washing over me, a feeling that's catching on from many of the other young soldiers-to-be. We were traveling further from Salem than we, ever in our lifetime, had expected to.

We reached the camp at Framingham an hour and a half later. The rainstorm that began that evening did not let up, and there was no place for us all to sleep except for in our pitched tents on fields behind Camp Whitney. No dinner was made ready for us there. We had to go without creature comforts for the whole night and into the next morning, but it was for Uncle Sam.

I have decided to keep a small journal, and to jot down my daily activities in it, so that I may, someday, be able to look back on this time of my life. It will be a kind of companion, I suppose,

21

and I will go to it in order to find some sense of security and comfort along this journey. I look at this situation with a definite mixture of excitement and apprehension. The bottom line is that I have to serve my country, and we are all here in the name of *honneur,* and to prove our bravery.

* * *

The following six days were filled with marching drills and inspections of the equipment. We were quickly becoming soldiers. On the third day of our time at in Framingham, the officers in charge decided to open up Camp Whitney to the public, and many people came across the field to see us in formation. Again, there was a mixture of feelings about this: on the one hand, I felt like a zoo animal, imprisoned, with folks gawking at me; but on the other hand, it was indeed exciting to be the center of so much fanfare.

The highlight of this week was when father made the trip to Camp Whitney by himself to visit. It was bittersweet. He was proud of me; but I could tell that he was also full of sorrow. His little boy had been suddenly catapulted into manhood, and the thought may have crossed his mind, that because of all of the uncertainties ahead, there is a chance that we may not see each other again. He came bearing gifts: first, a little package from our neighbor, Rose—a medal depicting Saint Christopher, and a perfumed card, on which she wrote that she said that she's awaiting my return to Story Street; and also, a long-sleeved knitted sweater to ensure that I would be warm enough, come winter. Our visit was abbreviated by the business of the day. I was a detail at the freight yard that morning, and then in the afternoon, after my visit with Pa, we all stood in line for a medical examination. I was immediately mustered into the Federal Service.

There was more rain. It rained the entire day. And I wondered: *Is this a foreshadowing of what we shall endure throughout the next weeks and months?* We broke camp on the field, waiting for a marching order; however, we did not move at all, and we ended the day of anticipation by sleeping at Camp Whitney for another night.

Only faintly aware of what day it was, we were ordered to leave the camp the next morning at sunrise. Our great adventure was now underway, on this 27th of June. Two hours later we all entrained at the Framingham station, bound for the Mexican border, via the Shore Line train. I sat flanked by Roland and Stanis, with my gear in the overhead storage compartment, and wondered about the future. We were all of the age when we felt that we were completely indestructible and utterly invulnerable. Our hearts were beating strong, not only with our youthful sense of adventure, but also with a dash of the adrenalin of 'fight or flight'.

* * *

Our journey by steam engine lasted seven days and six nights, with stops in Providence, New London, New Haven, Syracuse, Buffalo, Cleveland, Chicago, Alton, Kansas City, Santa Fe, Turnsdad, over Ratoon Pass, to Raton, Las Vegas, and finally, El Paso station. There were some highlights along the way, like when we were passing through Syracuse, and all of the engines in the freight yard there were blowing their whistles to beat the band. Those engineers must have known that we were on a mission for Uncle Sam. Seeing the Catskills was lovely. On a few occasions we were able to leave the train, like when we arrived in the Windy City, and were allowed to walk around the town for a while; and in Kansas City we emerged from the train, and then all descended upon a fruit stand near the depot. In all, we passed through a grand total of *twelve* of our great States.

Going west through Kansas and then through Colorado, on the Santa Fe Line, I began thinking of old 'home sweet home': cookouts, family gatherings with Aunt Alice at the piano, Rose's lovely voice singing *Au Clair de la Lune* . . . But on the seventh day, my twentieth birthday, after we detrained at the headquarters, and finally reached the camp near El Paso at Fort Bliss where we were all issued our hundred rounds of ammunition, the feelings of homesickness were shoved aside. Stanis and Roland, in a duet, quietly sang 'happy birthday' to me, and we felt the irony. The vistas of this landscape are so utterly foreign to us. We, Company H, were transported, in the matter of a week, to what could have been a new planet, altogether; so, this fact helps the longings for home to subside a little.

The Fourth of July brought no fanfare, no bonus, no fireworks, not one thing out of the ordinary. There were, rather, regular duties and routines to perform around the arid, sordid, solemn Camp Cotton. After having worked as detail to help build an incinerator, I stood guard that evening, on vigil for Uncle Sam's independence, and I did not feel free. We all had to put ourselves aside: I was not longer Joseph Lavoix, son of Placide and Ernestine; I was Private Lavoix of Company H, of the First Massachusetts Field Artillery.

*   *   *

Under the hot sun, camp duties and drills continued, and days of July came and went. We all rotated guard and detail duties. Despite these monotonies, we all quickly came to the realization that our lives were, indeed, in danger; for there were some instances when we were targets for snipers shooting at us from across the border, though none of us got hurt. I would stare at the black and white photo of Pancho Villa that was posted in the mess hall, and then think about how he pulled me from Salem into this desert-land. Although Roland and Stanis and I had always gone to church, weaned on the doctrine of the New Testament, herded by the Sisters of Assumption at the Saint Joseph's Church and School, like lambs, I did not feel the urge to pray here. I do not know what the good Lord has in store for us. My faith is being tested, and I feel that I am failing. This is not a place where I have the motivation to continue my faith in God-the-Almighty-Father. I am an automaton, going through the motions. This God-forsaken desert is drying out my heart.

Chapter Eight

The Bivouac

July 23, 1916

We were having a time at the Officers' Mess Hall, when someone ran in and called out: "Sniper fire, sniper fire!" All the lights went out at Fort Bliss, and Company H was ready to cross the border in four minutes flat.

The pitch blackness of the desert is much more intense than any Salem night I have ever seen. With the lights of our oil lanterns shining through the thick-as-molasses night, I saw the tail of my first coyote on the march toward Mexico. The ground is crusty and dry, and we have to dodge wiry bunches of mesquite grass as we go, so as not to trip. After walking with a pack of men for about a mile, the lieutenant ordered us to turn back. The threat had passed. We had not left El Paso.

Roland, Stanis and I usually try to stick together when we have to venture out of Camp Cotton, but we are inevitably separated by our duties. Roland always carries with him, wherever he goes, and a photograph of his girl back home, Jeannette. I carry my journal and a picture of Rose, Jeannette's younger sister. I look at her dark brown curls, her hazel eyes, I wonder if I will ever see her face again.

July 24, 1916

Today we had to break camp at Cotton, hike upon a *mesa*, and pitch camp there to support some others. These 'others' are Battery C of the 5th USA Artillery; they are 150 men strong from Connecticut. It was a great effort to transport the tents, food, water, and artillery up to this high point, under the scorching sun. We were perched only five miles from the border. I thought sure that I would catch a glimpse of Pancho Villa, himself, mounted on his horse.

September 28, 1916

By day and by night, hour by hour, we have not interrupted our vigil. There has been only the monotony of military drills for several hours a day; for our captains know that we are raw troops, with no experience on a battlefield. We have only—gradually and reluctantly—become fighting men. Today at noon, after we sat down to eat our beans and bread, we got the happy news that we would be heading back home. For a time, I let the longings for home—which I have been keeping at bay, lest they flood my heart—fill me.

Roland and I got permission to go into El Paso town to have a look around for an hour. On the El Paso-Juarez Souvenir Folder of postcards that I purchased to send home I wrote:

To: Placide Lavoix/ 38 Story Street/ Salem, MA
From: Joseph Lavoix/ Company H, 8th Regt. Mass/ El Paso, Texas

> *Chers Parents,*
> *Je vous envoie quelques vues d'ici que j'ai de la ville.*
> *De salut de toute la famille,*
> *—Joseph.*
> *PS: J'ai collé ce petit papier parce que je me suis trompé d'adresse.*

[dear Parents,
I am sending you some views of here that I have of the city.
Greetings to the whole family.
—Joseph.
PS: I glued on this little piece of paper because I wrote
the wrong address.

After dinner came the crushing announcement that we were called for a campaign into New Mexico in order to serve as reinforcements for the troops at Fort Selden in Las Cruces, and for this we would leave in two days' time. In the meantime, my detail this evening is to build another outhouse, which means there is a lot of digging and more digging into the dry earth. This is no longer an adventure if it ever was one; it is surely an *ordeal*.

October 12, 1916

Rumor has it that the men of Company H will be replaced by those of Company G, the National Guardsmen from Georgia. We will be able to pack our belongings and return to New England on Saturday. I will not believe this until it really happens. I do not want to cause myself any unnecessary heartache.

Over the past two weeks, I witnessed several men and mules die from overexertion and heat stroke while on the Las Cruces expedition. We traveled a total of 100 miles on foot. I wonder if Black Jack knows of the toll of the death of one man on his family and friends. And I wonder: has he gotten a hold of his *Señor* Villa yet?

Four men and five mules perished, after two days of hiking, on the way to Anthony from Latima, Texas. We laid their parched bodies to rest alongside of the road, for we had no way of carrying them with us. The sun's power is so intense and so urgent: the soil covering the bodies quickly became bone dry, even though it had come from darker realms beneath the crusty surface. I suppose that it's no coincidence that these men and beasts died on the way to Las Cruces, which I learned means "the crosses" in Spanish. The irony is that their graves are without crosses, so this place should be renamed *Sin Cruces.*

At Mesquite, New Mexico, on the fourth day of our expedition, our feet were swollen to beat the band, and we were still only half way between Anthony and Las Cruces. That night we pitched camp near Mesquite, and again, I was detail to an outhouse. On Day Five we passed by the old Fort Fillmore at Mesilla Park, and finally arrived at Fort Selden which is north of Las Cruces town. I was on the rear guard, and it was *some* job; though the Captain did thank us for our hard work. Day Six: We awoke with a view of Black Mountain in the distance, and just as we were getting into formation, the order came from our Captain that we would have to turn on our heels and head back to Camp Cotton. On Day Seven we did not rest, as the Good Lord did; instead we departed at seven in the morning, and we made it to Anthony where we were met with a sandstorm, but had to pitch out tents there, nonetheless. The beans I ate for dinner tasted like soap. On Day Eight we encountered another storm on the way from Anthony to the Borderland Inn which is near the town of Santa Teresa, this time it was a rainstorm which soaked us to the skin. By nighttime we were all, unusually, very cold, but had to keep working; I was on a water detail, others were loading up the wagons. On the ninth day we finally reached Camp Cotton, glad and happy, but tired. The band played a round of patriotic tunes to welcome us.

I now have the courage to send another Souvenir Folder of picture postcards to Ma and Pa. This time they are color illustrations of a Mexican bullfight and other characteristic scenes in Mexico:

> *Chers Parents —*
> *Je vous envoie quelques vues du fameux Mexico. C'est ici que vous voyez des mexicains. On est à seulement 50 pas du border. Ils nous regardent et on les regarde. J'ai hâté d'aller au devant d'eux autres. Je voudrais leur si belle moustache.*

Roland, Stanis et moi, nous sommes ensemble encore une
fois.
De votre fils, — Joseph.

[Dear Parents,
I am sending you some views of famous Mexico. It is
here that you can see some Mexicans. We are only 50
paces from the border. They look at us and we look at
them. I hastened to get in front of the others [to have a
look at them]. I would like to have their very beautiful
mustache.
Roland, Stanis and I are together once again.
From your son, —Joseph.]

When we got back to Camp Cotton afterward, the train cars,
29 in all, were ready for us in the station. In the morning we will
be on our way.

Chapter Nine

Entrenched

Fort Vaux, Verdun, le 4 juillet, 1916

Chère Maman,

Tu sais combien coûte une guerre? Je crois que la somme ne peut pas être calculée. Ici à Verdun, après quatre mois de combat, c'est le prix de la perte d'une vie humaine fois trois cents mille vies. Ce chiffre ne peut pas être sondé.

Nous sommes très fatiqués, mais nous avons des commandes du Général Nivelle. Ils nous dit: "Vous ne les laisserez pas passer, mes camarades!" Il faut les battre, même s'il y du gaz. Oui, ils nous gasent—avec de la chlore, de la moutarde, du phosgène, et maintenant du diphosgène. Le paysage ressemble à un Armageddon du vingtième siècle.

Et notre voisin, Michel, est tombé à cause du gaz. Ça, c'est le prix d'une guerre. Et cela coûte trop cher: et quel est le prix de la vie de Michel fois trois cents mille??

Ton,
—Philippe.

* * *

Vaux Fort, Verdun, July 4, 1916

Dear Mom,

Do you know how much a war costs? I believe that the sum cannot be calculated. Here in Verdun, after four months of combat, it is the cost of the loss of one life, times three hundred thousand lives. This number cannot be fathomed.

We are very tired, but we have General Nivelle's orders. He says to us: "You shall not let them pass, my comrades!" We have to fight them, even if there is now gas. Yes, they are gassing us—with chlorine, mustard, phosgene and now diphosgene. The landscape looks like an Armageddon of the twentieth century.

And our neighbor, Michel, fell from the gas. That is the price of a war. And that is too expensive: and what is the price of the life of Michel times three hundred thousand??

Yours,
—*Philippe.*

Chapter Ten
A Letter from Montaigu

Montaigu, le 11 octobre, 1916

Cher Philippe,

Je compte les jours et les nuits de ton absence: ça fait cinq cents sept jours et cinq cents huit nuits de vide depuis ta dernière—ta seule—visite à la maision, et tu me manques. Je m'inquiète, souvent, de ce que tu as à subir dans les tranchées et au champ de bataille, et je me demande si on ne sera jamais capable de se remettre de tels essais. J'aimerais bien t'aider à te remettre quand tu rentres chez toi, chez nous, si c'est possible.

La guerre dirige nos vies, ici, aussi. Je suis des études d'infirmière maintenant, et je vais aller travailler dans un hôpital militaire près de Paris au mois de janvier, aussitôt que je finesse mes examens. Je sais qu'il y a un besoin d'infirmières près du champs de bataille parce qu'il y a des reclames affichés par le gouvernement aux babillards à l'université. Je vais faire ma part pour cette guerre.

Ici à La Vendée, il n'y a plus de jeunes hommes, car il sont soit partis pour la lutte dans les tranchées, soit déjà partis pour aller voir le bon Dieu. On avait vraiment tort de penser que la guerre aurait été terminée avant Noël de 1914. On n'a jamais prévu qu'elle va durer aussi longtemps . . .

Je sais que tu vas rentrer sain et sauf à la maison un jour bientôt. Je sais que cette guerre terrible se terminera, même si elle semble à tout le monde qu'elle va s'éterniser. Même de loin, je peux sentir la douleur provoquée par le conflit. Le gouvernement veut garder le moral de tout le monde élévé, pour continuer la lutte; il veut nous protéger des réalités de la guerre. Mais je sais comment il est vraiment: tu regardes tes amis tués par des tirs, des grenades, et maintenant le gaz. Tu as peu de temps pour faire le deuil de leur perte. Tu es blessé, et tes blessures ont besoin de soin. Tu as froid, et tu dois faire face à toutes sortes de vermines dans les tranchées—les poux, les rats, etc . . . Tu sens l'odeur de la mort tout autour. Telles sont les réalités d'une guerre. Je sais que cela doit être comme l'Enfer, même.

Sais que tu nous manques tellement, et que nous attendons ton retour à la maison.

Avec tout le coeur,
—Monique.

*   *   *

Montaigu, October 11, 1916

Dear Philippe,

I am counting the days and nights of your absence: it has been five hundred seven days and five hundred seven nights of emptiness since your last—your only—visit home, and I miss you. I worry often about what you have to go through in the trenches and on the battlefield, and I wonder whether one will ever be able to recover from such trials. I would really like to help you recover when you return home, if that is possible.

The war directs our lives here, too. I am now studying Nursing, and I am going to go work in a military hospital near

Paris in January, as soon as I finish my exams. I know that there is a need for nurses near the battlefields because there are advertisements posted by the government on the message boards at the university. I am going to do my part for this war.

There are no young men left here in La Vendée anymore, because they have all either left for the battle in the trenches, or have departed to go to see the Lord. One was really wrong to have thought that this war would be over before Christmas of 1914. One never foresaw that it would last so long.

I know that you will make it back at home safely someday soon. I know that this dreadful War will end, even though it seems to everyone that it will drag on forever. Even from afar, I can feel the pain that this conflict is causing everyone. The government wants to keep everyone's morale high, to continue the fight; they want to shield the realities of war from us at the home front. But I know how it really is: you watch your friends being killed by gunfire, grenades, and now gas. You have little time to mourn their loss. You are injured, and your wounds need care. You are cold, and must contend with all kinds of vermin in the trenches—rats, lice, etc . . . . You smell the odor of death all around you. These are the realities of a war. I know that it is what Hell, itself, must be like.

Please know that you a sorely missed by everyone here, and that we all await your return home.

With all my heart,
—Monique.

Chapter Eleven

The Return

I cannot believe that I am going home. I will see lovely Forest River Park, hear the cry of seagulls again at Palmer's Cove, smell the popped corn at the Willows, taste Mother's pea soup and *creton*, and finally relax on our Story Street porch with sweet Rose at my side. I cannot believe it. The Santa Fe Line rolls us closer and closer to Home Sweet Home.

My last duty on the Mexican border was as a sentry, on guard at the outpost. *Amen!* Orders to pack up our belongings sent us all to work with great pleasure; there was an ease to all of our activities that day. Even our last drill at El Paso, which was only two hours long, seemed effortless.

At dawn the next day came the most welcomed sight: the men from Georgia of Company G. We gave them all three good cheers! While they were settling in, we were at work dismantling our tents and stuffing our barrack bags. The last of the rituals of Camp Cotton were performed on that day: we stood retreat. At the pitch black hour of two-in-the-morning on the following day we left the camp behind. *Adieu, Pancho Villa! Adieu, Black Jack!*

The 29 freight cars at the El Paso Station stretched on for what appeared to be a half a mile, and Richard and I boarded one together, with Roland further up. There was, however, a long delay of over twelve hours; I did not know why. As steam engines huffed and puffed, our train pulled out of El Paso town on the eve of the 29th, rolling at first slowly on its great steel wheels, then gradually gaining in speed. The train whistle sounded, and clusters of mesquite trees whizzed by. I thought that I was dreaming; for me, it was at *that* moment that the adventure began.

At Fort Hancock, located about an hour away, we made a brief stop. Looking forlorn, the soldiers there greeted us; and perhaps out of envy, they told us that we would all end up returning to Texas in about a month or so. At this, some disappointment and a little fear filled me, but I shrugged it off. I felt more alert and much freer to take in the sights, sounds, and smells around me at this point of the campaign. I knew that I was moving closer and closer to personal freedoms. And now the landscape and the atmosphere—which had, heretofore, caused much annoyance and even fear—fascinated and impressed me. Our freight cars soon rumbled precariously over the enormous Amistad Canyon, on a train bridge named Big Ben that stretched over a mile long and stood 365 feet over the rushing water and auburn rocks, and it shook like the devil as we rolled on. It was *some* sight to see. These were some of the funniest looking rocks that we had ever seen yet. We were able to get out of the freight car and walk around a bit when we arrived at Del Rio town, where we stopped for two hours to change engines and to take some water. Gee whiz, was it *warm* out there.

I met a fellow from Portland, Maine when we passed through San Antonio, voyaging east, across the southern part of the Lone Star State on our way to New Orleans. He said to me that it was very cold in Chicago and snowing in Massachusetts, and this contrast to arid Texas-lands was amazing to us. I also encountered a soldier who was carrying an armadillo, whom he had adopted as his pet, which was exotic to me. I saw a cotton field for the first time in my life on the last day of October, shortly before we arrived in Houston: stretching on for several acres, until they met the flat horizon, were large green leaves, spotted with puffs of white here-and-there. I found it to be quite lovely: I had never seen so much green. I knew at this point that there would be many 'firsts' for us on this trek back to our hometown.

Houston—which is a swell place, better place than El Paso—is a growing city. We were again allowed to detrain and walk around the town a bit. Impressive was the sight of a 22-story building on a beautiful street. But we had to move like hell, and be back on time for the roll call. Other points of interest—all still in Texas, heading eastward—were Dayton, Liberty, Beaumont and Orange. Most eye-catching, while passing through these territories, were the lengthy bridges: on one, stretching about three quarters of a mile long, we passed over quicksand and water, and then there was another and another, both draw bridges, and very long. Orange is a swell little town, but once we passed it, making our way toward Louisiana, there was an odor coming into the cars, and we had to close every window. *At last* we left Texas. I had been there for four long months. I hope I don't see it ever again.

* * *

New Orleans is a mule town, I noticed. The ferry on the Mississippi River from Algiers Point took us across it, into the city center, and we had a look around. It was the first of November, and warm. What I liked most about this fine city was the Saint Patrick's Church. It is the prettiest church I have ever seen in my life yet. On a plaque I read that it was built in the 'Gothic' style; it had a very tall church tower. It was mighty good to feel like a tourist, after so many months of training and drills in the field. The Court House and the Central Fire Station were some of the other points of interest. An old Veteran from Massachusetts was very glad to see us, and we all smiled at each other and conversed with him a little. What surprised me most when passing through this town was to see a woman who, as she boarded the train with us, on the journey eastward toward Mississippi and Alabama, was *smoking a pipe*.

From the "toe" of the "boot" of Louisiana at New Orleans, our train continued hugging the Gulf, and carried us over the swamps passing Ocean Springs, Mississippi. Here, a field of orange trees spread out before us, and it was a pretty sight. I can only compare this to a forest of red maple trees in a late autumn in New England. Then, at last, the engine swung northward, and the ascent to the Northeast began. This was a very good feeling, euphoric even; though, still, it did not seem real to me that I was going home. By nightfall we were in Mobile, Alabama—where we stopped for short time to change engines and obtain water. The dry dock at Mobile was a sight to see: it looked like a giant-sized swimming pool with the water drained out of it. Thomaston was also a great place, with a population of only 800. Note: from El Paso to New Orleans, 1,100 miles; from New Orleans to Montgomery, 318 miles; from Montgomery to Nashville, 310 miles.

As the sun was rising on the second day of November, we passed through Birmingham Station, which, I learned, is home to the biggest saw mill in the world. Boy, I saw *some* woodcutter in Birmingham. Boyles was the next beautiful town, and there they make locomotives, cars, boats, and so forth. It is also home to the Birmingham Steel Mine. So, this is steel mill and iron mining country, I determined. Our engine then pulled us, due north, through Decatur and over the Tennessee River. From our freight car we watched how bales of cotton are carried by teams of horses, and then the teams are driven *into* the river, and the cotton is loaded onto big rafts to be transported to towns and cities up river. That was *some* sight. I think touring around like this a good way to learn about the world without reading books about it all. At high noon we crossed the Tennessee line.

Our dinner was too sweet, so we threw it out of the window, alongside of the track. I will always remember this day at Carnesville; it was a great time. We were soon at Nashville, and detrained to have a look around. I saw the reservoir, the Y.M.C.A., the Capitol building, and, of course, the train depot. It was *some* depot, being three stories high. There were two Privates absent at roll call: Jerry Cornwell and Sullivan. But we rolled on without them, through East Nashville and over the Cumberland River, arriving at Louisville just before midnight. Louisville is *some* place.

The third day of November was spent in the state of Ohio: Cincinnati, Columbus, and Cleveland. At the Kentucky-Ohio border, still in Kentucky, we spied the Latonia Race Track, the biggest in the US. This adds to my growing knowledge of national trivia. At Cincinnati, we broke a window, so we had to wait in the station at bit. Private Moreau and I teamed up against Rich and his partner for a game of cards, and Moreau and I beat the pants off them. I noticed that there are trains that run on the streets, and this was another 'first' for me. At Columbus, we had an hour to ourselves, so Roland and I made the most of our 'tourist' time in this city. Some sights we saw were the Statehouse, the impressive statue of McKinley, and the jail. Many squirrels frolicked among us in front of the Statehouse. I was surprised that they were not fearful of people, like they are in Salem. I suppose that they're used to people around, and also know that we provide food. This reminded me of a time in Haverhill two years ago. Note: Nashville to Cincinnati, 350 miles; Cincinnati to Columbus, 120 miles.

At the end of this Ohio Day, we arrived in Cleveland at five minutes before twelve midnight; that's five before one, Boston time. We learned that there was a big fire somewhere, and we had some rain which we hadn't seen for *weeks*. In Cleveland the machine shops are working night and day.

On the seventh day of our journey home, it was still raining and very cold in the early morning hours. I calculated then that it would only be two more days of travel until we reached Boston. It was a kind of restful day: we passed the time playing checkers and cards. A sight I won't forget while in transit from Cleveland to Buffalo was a freight train loaded with apples: there were "mountains" of apples. I have never seen so many apples in my life. I suppose that they were New York apples since we had just crossed the Pennsylvania-New York border, and were fast approaching the city of Buffalo. At Lackawanna, after passing over a brand new bridge, we saw a big dock. Not far from the dock, was a big railroad freight yard, where goods from all over are loaded from the ships onto trains, and vice versa, from trains onto the ships, and then transported to other destinations. This is the biggest freight yard I have seen yet. Information about the sights travels among the soldiers, so I learned that steamers from all parts of the country land here. Only three miles out of Buffalo Junction and I saw another new bridge. Talk about bridges! They have the biggest bridgework there. Note: from Columbus to Cleveland, 124 miles; from Cleveland to Buffalo, 239 miles.

An enormous, rectangular warehouse-looking building that stretches for at least 400 yards came into site. This lamb tanner factory at Buffalo Junction looks like the United Shoe Company in Beverly. And a lumber yard sprawled out in the distance before us from the freight cars. It was *some* lumber yard. I would say that Buffalo-on-the-Erie is a city of much commerce and trade. We were able to see only the outskirts of the place beginning at high noon, and then, a few hours later, just before sunset, we were on our way once again. Ten miles out from Buffalo, we were impressed by a big car shop at a place called Dellwood. From here onward, there was an especially playful and jovial air in the train, for we knew that we would soon be greeted by our family members and friends.

Rochester is a beautiful city. We had the chance to visit this lovely place for about an hour, when we walked through the park that lay along the river. It was very green, and the air was so fresh. The people seemed to be very pleasant. Back on the freight, we chugged on through the rest of the great state of New York, past Syracuse, and by the time we reached Rotterdam, we were well into the eighth day of our journey. It was at Rotterdam Junction that we all transferred to a double header—to two Boston-and-Maine engines; and believe me, we traveled a long distance for a while afterward. It was good to say *adieu* to the Santa

Fe Line cars. Note: Buffalo to Syracuse, 160 miles; from Syracuse to Rochester, 80 miles; Rotterdam to Boston, 203 miles.

A flock of pheasants and a big herd of sheep seemed to greet us from the fields as we passed over Eagle Bridge, through a little place called Hoosae Junction, New York. We soon saw the first snow of the year atop the mountains in the state of Vermont, the white caps stretching on for miles and miles. Next, we came upon a tunnel that passed for miles under the mountains in the western part of Massachusetts. Roland timed the passage: he clocked it as sixteen minutes and 27 seconds, and a distance of four-and-three-quarter miles. The ground below us was white when we emerged from the tunnel. It seemed that we had passed into a new land; for before entering the tunnel, it had been raining . . . We felt like Alice moving down the rabbit hole! Greenfield, ironically, was our next stop, with two inches of snow on the ground, and I thought of that man in San Antonio who had told us that there was already snowfall in our home state. We had an hour to ourselves in the town, so we fetched our barrack bags and had a walk around to stretch our legs. At Fitchburg the top told us that we would be in Boston at six o'clock, sharp. Further instructions were that we would have six hours off once we got there, and then we would have to report back for roll call at midnight.

Boston was our next stop. We made it. We made it there before eight o'clock. Corporal LaCombe and I skipped off to Salem on a regional train for a few hours, and then reported back to the Company before midnight. We slept on the train that night, and come morning, we awoke to the call to get in formation. We were to parade across the city from South Station to North. There was much fanfare and general jubilation. On that November 6th, the ninth day of our return, at ten to two, we all boarded the regional train for Dear Old Salem. We arrived at the Salem Depot at four o'clock. I never saw such a happy bunch of people in the depot yet. We unloaded our barrack bags, and then watched the train pull out with Company G, off for Gloucester. The parade through Salem was a final, symbolic salute: the citizens of Salem saluted

41

us, and we, the soldiers, saluted them back. The parade finished in front of the Salem Armory in the center of town. There was a formal dismissal. I simply walked to Story Street from there, my body feeling very light. A good, square meal was waiting for me at home.

Chapter Twelve
The Toll

Fort Vaux, Verdun
le 24 décembre, 1916

Chère Maman,

 Tu ne pourrais pas reconnaître ton fils, si tu avais l'occasion de me rendre visite ici. Je ne me reconnais plus, non plus. On nous appelle maintenant "les poilus", car chacun de nous, les soldats, a besoin de rendre visite au barbier . . .

 Comment est-ce que je peux te communiquer combien cette lutte pour la terre française est abominable?? Il y a tantes de situations affreuses, tants de camarades perdus, tantes d'atrocités, que les mots ne viennent pas à la bouche afin de décrire les scènes que ton fils a eu à témoigner. Et souvent, nous avons faim et nous avons soif, et nous avons froid. Et, simplement dit, nous avons peur. Les difficultés physiques—les mains et les pieds gelés, les poux aux cheveux, le bruit, et le gaz—nous empêchent de garder un esprit sain. En plus, les champs de bataille sont tellement abîmés, tellement déformés par les explosions des mines terrestres que la terre ressemble à une sorte d'endroit extraterrestre. C'est une topographie des cratères.

La bataille a fini, mais la guerre misérable continue. Tu sais que l'histoire se répète? Le mot "Verdun" même veut dire "fort fort". En 1792, quand les prussiens sont venus, ils ont battu les forces révolutionnaires françaises, et donc la porte à Paris est devenue ouverte. Mais cette-fois-ci, la deuxième fois, on verra. Les "prussiens" ne verront pas la capitale.

Je sais que vous — toi et Papa — faites le meilleur effort possible de contribuer votre énérgie à ce combat pour la Patrie; que vous envoyez à l'Armée ce que vous avez récolté de la terre. Les nouvelles qui arrivent au front nous disent que les citoyens de chaque coin de la France font leur part pour la cause de la guerre, et ces nouvelles remontent le moral.

Sera-t-il un "joyeux" Noël? Puis-je vous envoyer telles voeux, quand je sais bien qu'il n'y a rien de joyeux à propos de cette Nuit Sainte ici à Fort Vaux? Néanmoins, je vous envoie ce petit cadeau, ce paquet de dragées — une specialité de Verdun. La cloche sonne maintenant, et on va à la messe de minuit avec les autres croyants.

Ton fils,
— Philippe

*   *   *

Fort Vaux, Verdun
December 24, 1916

Dear Mom,

You would not be able to recognize your son if you had the chance to visit me here. I don't recognize myself, either. People call us "the hairy ones" now because each one of us, the soldiers, needs to pay a visit to the barber.

How can I communicate to you how much this struggle for French soil is abominable? There are so many horrible situations, so many lost comrades, so many atrocities that words do not come to one's mouth to describe the scenes that your son has had to witness. And often, we are hungry and we are thirsty, and we are cold. And simply put, we are afraid. The physical difficulties—our frozen hands and feet, the noise, and the gas—prevent us from keeping a healthy mind. On top of this, the battlefields are so damaged, so deformed by the landmine explosions, that the earth looks some kind of extraterrestrial place. It is topography of craters.

The battle has come to an end, but the miserable war continues. Do you know that history is repeating itself? The word "Verdun" itself means "strong fort"; and it has been a place of conflict before. In 1792, when the Prussians came, and defeated the French Revolutionary forces, the door to Paris was opened. But this time, the *second* time, we shall see. The "Prussians" will not see the Capital.

I know that you—you and Dad—are making the best effort possible to contribute your energy to this fight for the fatherland; that you're sending what you harvest from the land to the Army. The news that arrives at the front tells us that citizens from each corner of France are doing their part for the cause of the war, and this news lifts our spirits.

Will it be a "merry" Christmas? Can I send such wishes, all the while knowing that there is nothing merry about this Holy Night here at Fort Vaux? Nevertheless, I am sending you this little gift, this little package of *dragées*—a specialty of Verdun. The bells are now tolling, and we're off to midnight mass with the others.

Your son,
—*Philippe.*

Chapter Thirteen
Family

Pa now works long hours at the mills. At quitting time, many of his peers go to the local bar on Dow Street, but my father comes home to rest; for he wants to make a good life for my mother, and for what is left of our family. He wants a peaceful life. Conversing with relatives and neighbors in the parlor, especially after church on Sunday afternoons, and woodworking are his pastimes. He is very talented craftsman; with care, he recently built a fine wooden chest with an adjustable drawer in which he stores his hand tools. He is a quiet man who has already had more than his share of adversity, and I can see that he has managed difficulties with hard work, grace, and humility.

Placide is his given name, which in French means "peaceful", but I know that it is not an apt description of way he has lived so far. My father left his home in Trois Rivières, Québec when he was only twelve years old, and after that he was never to see his parents again. His father was among the ninth generation of French inhabitants of 'New France'; and his grandmother—as family legend goes—was a member of the Algonquin tribe, and she could lift and carry heavy bundles with ease. So, Placide and his three siblings were known as 'mixed breeds'. The first European settlers of New France were my ancestors who hailed from Normandy and La Vendée; some traveled over the Atlantic with Maisonneuve almost four hundred years ago. Although Placide has never seen France, he speaks fluent French. The language of his ancestors is part of his very being, and continues to be passed along to each new generation.

The life of a subsistence farmer had no appeal to Pa, and anyway, land was scarce, so he joined the wave of a million *Francos* who made their way south. It was the fashionable thing to do: to go to America and to find work in the mills of the river towns of New England, at a time when southern Québec was suffering from a severe economic depression. A teenager, he arrived in South Salem, alone, after working for a year or two in the timber industry in Maine. Immediately, he found work in the textile mills; namely, at the Naumkeag Steam Cotton Company, also known as the 'Pequot Mills', on Congress Street. He is a sheets and pillowcases manufacturer. I find it ironic that the mills were named after the Indian tribe that had occupied the area for many hundreds of years before the coming of the Europeans.

Pa was a handsome young man, with a clear complexion, olive-colored skin, an aquiline nose. He made his way, living modestly on the low wages paid to the thousands of French-Canadian mill hands, most of who arrived in this land a generation ago. Then, on a clear day in South Salem, he met my mother, Mademoiselle Boulanger. I have met only five of my nine siblings. Marie, Arthur, Gracie, and Elida all passed away before I could get to know who they were. Noel died at the age of four. The illnesses of our time—which cannot, as yet, be prevented or cured—are pertussis and diphtheria. Three brothers and one sister are left to me: René, Valère, and Rosario—whom we call 'Pete', and Florida. The loss of so many of my siblings has taken its toll on my kind parents. I can see the corners of their mouths turn down after the loss of each child, each time the gravity of it all seems to pull them a little lower.

My mother, Ernestine, is strong-willed and magnanimous, yet her mettle has been tested at every turn. Like most French Catholic woman, she is encouraged to have many children to support the parish, and to establish the French culture in this adopted country: this is known as the second *révolution des berceaux* — 'revolution of the cradles'. Within nine years, she has given birth to ten children. She has outlived five of them. Although she knows that she is not alone in this situation, I don't think that the pain of losing her children is lessened with this knowledge. A sadness fills her eyes, which has come with having to say 'goodbye' to my siblings, one-by-one. Without the Church as her foundation, without her strong faith, she would not be able to live on. The work that has to be done to maintain a household with five children keeps her going, too.

My father cannot read English, but he keeps an ear to the ground for the news of the day; for he is a 'foreigner' in this land, and wishes to stay informed. He is our source of news about the outside world, because no one else in the family has the inclination to listen as he does. He has told us about the war that is going on in Europe right now. He tells us about the atrocities committed by the Germans against the French, about the standoff in the trenches on French soil, and about the industry and tactics of war, developed now by both sides—the land mines, gas warfare, gunfire, bayonets, and of the misery of life in the trenches. About all of this he learns from neighbors, friends and co-workers. America wants to help, but from a distance. President Wilson was just re-elected for another four years in office. People like him because he has kept the United States out of the war so far. So many other countries of the world have already joined in: England, Belgium, Russia, and many others, so it seems that the rest of the world is in the grips of this terrible fight. My father says the President wants all parties engaged in the war to stop fighting. He has recently called for "peace without victory", but they will not have it. Placide does not live in peaceful times.

* * *

René and I now go to work with my father at the Mills every day; our shift begins at seven o'clock, and we finish at five. We are not the youngest ones on-the-job; some mill hands are only thirteen, and they are dwarfed by the size of the looms. When we hear the final bell of the day, we make the five-minute walk home, to be greeted by mother and our *souper*: the house smells of pea soup and salty ham and pepper. In good times, there is also a fresh loaf of bread from Audet's on the table, and this one of the simple pleasures that my father savors.

Florida just finished school, and although she is only fourteen, she has started working at Desjardin's Jewelers on Essex Street, earning a dollar and fifty cents per day. Because our parents need the money to pay back their loan to the credit union, we have all had to finish up our schooling in the eighth grade, and then find a paid job. Valère has one more year at Saint Joseph's, and then he will have to join us at our looms. Because he so enjoys his studies, and he is a very good student—the sisters always send home their notes of praise—this is really a shame. Little Pete has a few more years to go. If he is lucky—that is, if there's enough money coming in—then he will be able to continue on and finish secondary school. This will be a family first.

On Saturdays, when we finally feel free, René and I take long walks along the railroad tracks that are parallel to Canal Street, and beyond, to collect pieces of coal that fall from the Boston & Maine locomotives. Our hands become very black after doing this for a couple of hours, but we are able to come home with a canvas bag filled with fuel for the stove in the basement, and this always makes our parents smile. The next stop is the Woods and the Great Swamp beyond Castle Hill, further along the railroad tracks. They are our refuge. We spend hours there, pretending we are professional Scouts. René makes a very good campfire, and sometimes we roast potatoes pulled from the *potager* upon it. And if he has managed to find any cigarettes during his travels, then he plucks one out of his jacket pocket and has a smoke. We have cut several trails in these woods, just as the

49

Pequots did before us, and we enjoy it more than anything else. I often wonder if we enjoy these woods so much because of our Indian ancestors, and I wonder at the same time what my great grandmother looks like, and what her Algonquin life in Canada is like. My father doesn't speak about her very much.

Chapter Fourteen
The Call

René and I were covered with burs, and gleaming with perspiration when we returned home from our overnight expedition in the Woods. Cool temperatures met the hour of the sunrise, and from our bed of moss under the oak trees we breathed in the fresh air with a smile upon our faces. But then the summer day burst forth, and the impact of it was even harder once we emerged from the forest, and walked upon the gravel of the streets of Castle Hill. We exited the woods feeling like professional Adventurers, our minds and imaginations refreshed and nourished from a night spent under the stars; but as we walked toward home, the feeling melted away: the heat was just too oppressive.

We did not have to be at our looms at the Mills, since we had a two week recess, and for this we were very grateful; for we would not have to be submitted to the almost unbearable heat inside the factory. Yes, the mercury read 96 degrees, so we called on Rose and her sister, and headed to Lynn Beach with a shoulder bag stuffed with *creton* sandwiches and potato chips, and we felt lucky—lucky to have each other, and lucky to have the day off. It was a day of ocean breezes and body surfing.

My luck ran out on this mid-summer Wednesday. The call came during supper, just like the last time. At the Armory I would see Corporal LaCombe and the other members of Company H of the 8th Massachusetts Field Artillery once again. My breath was cut short, as if I had had the wind knocked out of me, and my heartbeat quickened. This time, I felt more a feeling of panic than the last time; for last year there was also a sense of euphoria and adventure. I know that once again I am called to fulfill my "duty" in the name of honor, and I know that I have to muster what I can from within, and mask this feeling of panic that has arisen in me. Last night, under the stars, I dreamed of a beautiful future with Rose at my side. I dreamed of more excursions in the Woods, and, perhaps, one day, a trip to New Hampshire with my family and friends . . .

I know what's happening in the world beyond Salem, because Pa always talks about 'the Great War' at supper and at the Sunday afternoon parlor hour, but all the trouble seemed so far away from Story Street, until today. I know that President Wilson declared war on Germany back in April, even though he won a second term in office in November because he 'kept us out of the war.' Now we're in: 'to keep the world safe for democracy'. We've taken the side of the "Allied Powers", and that means that I will have to go to France. For now, our bodies are stuck at the Salem Armory, but our minds are racing.

October 29, 1917

We stayed at the Armory for four days, and on the fourth day we moved to Camp Housten in Lynnfield, where we stayed for almost the whole month of August. Rose came to visit me on my last day in Lynnfield, and we promised that we would write to each other. She is *some* girl. Others came the day before to say 'goodbye': Ma and Pa, René, Valère, Florida, little Pete, and also our neighbors, the Audets and the Deschenes. I did not cry, but I really felt very downhearted. I have no idea when I will see everyone again.

Near the end of August, we entrained for Camp Bartlett in Westfield. It was a difficult trip because we had to stay in the train cars overnight, even though the ride to the western part of the state took only three hours. Once we arrived at the Camp, our Company was mixed up with the 2nd Massachusetts Field Artillery, so we were issued the wrong gear in the confusion. Day-after-day, it was the same routine for us; there were endless drills and orders to carry out. I stuck close to the other Salem boys—Roland and Rich, and we spent our free time together, whenever there was any. We all knew that Westfield was a 'holding station', and that, at some point soon, we would have to make the trans-Atlantic voyage by ship, though we were all in-the-dark about the travel details.

Roused from our slumber before sun-up, at four hundred hours, October sixth, we embarked on the trip north to Montréal by train. It was at Montréal that we boarded the famous *SS Scotian*, like lemmings, bound for Halifax, and we left Montréal that Sunday evening at six. Since there were so many of us, we were put down in steerage, among the rats, without any lights. The highlight of that part of the journey was the time spent on deck, passing by the great city of Québec as we sailed along the mighty Saint Lawrence River. We saw that famous bridge, *le Pont de Québec*, and we all thought that the ship would not be able to pass under it, but it did, without complication. It was *some* sight.

Halifax was our next stop, three days later, where the ship hands took more supplies on board for the journey ahead. When we pulled into port at eight o'clock that morning, we were able to venture out of the ship only briefly, and with our small allowance, we purchased some dried herring to taste . . . . good, but very salty, like the ocean water! It was at this juncture that we learned that there would be an estimated eight to ten days at sea before we reached the next port at Liverpool, England. So, from Halifax, the ship pulled away from the Canadian coast on the fourteenth day of October. We do not know what is to become of us.

The ship was so damp, and also cold. We did our best to keep ourselves occupied while on board, so as to: 1) avoid being down in steerage, and 2) avoid the cold when on deck. Rich and Roland and I would meet each other to do calisthenics—push-ups, sit-ups, and jumping jacks whenever we could, besides helping out with regular duties, including cleaning and cooking tasks. An alarm went off at one thirty in the morning, after six days at sea in the early morning hours of the 20th. We all had to go up on deck with our life-saver jackets on for an unannounced, special drill. It was *some* night, and I won't forget it!

We all thought we'd be on this God-forsaken ship forever. There was a fair amount of sea sickness and homesickness among us and, of course, the fear of the unknown, which we tried to keep at bay by playing cards, when we could. I tried to just take things day by day. Nine days at sea, and the *SS Scotian* finally docked at port in Liverpool. We stayed on board the ship until the next morning, when we entrained on a steam engine bound for Southampton. To be walking on land once again felt almost unreal. It was raining to beat hell when we arrived at the next port, after dark, at twenty-one hundred hours. We were brought to and held at a rest camp. Southampton was our temporary home for five long days.

Yesterday was a very long day: I have named it 'English Channel Day'. It was high noon when we left the rest camp for the dock, and where we milled about for several hours. At seventeen hundred hours, we embarked on the fastest ship parked here; but again, there was the familiar Waiting Game. It was another several hours before leaving port in the late evening, to make the trip across the Channel.

We all did not sleep for long, but during my sleep last night I had a vivid dream: I was surrounded by my family back in Salem, and they were looking up at me; for I was standing on some hill. And—it was so strange—I was surprised that they, dressed in their Sunday best, all bowed low before me. They told that I would some day free them from their misery and fears, and from their hardships. They said I would lead my family into a more peaceful life . . . From this vantage point, it hardly seems at all possible. As I and the men of the 104th Infantry battle bouts of seasickness, all I see around me is ocean—stretched to the horizon. Am I still dreaming?

This morning, before sun-up, we landed in France, at a place called *Le Havre*. It was not yet five in the morning. And, as it turns out, it has been yet another day of waiting and more waiting for orders to leave the ship and to entrain, *car nom de Dieu*. Finally, we left Le Havre by train at ten o'clock at night, bound for we know-not-where. We had one meal in 41 hours.

Chapter Fifteen
Training

I was picked to work as an Interpreter, because I can speak French. This happened just ten days after our arrival in France. The job pays pretty well—eleven dollars a week—and I spend a lot of time riding around in trucks with officers, instead of doing details around camp. There are a lot of French girls who want to get to know me, too, but my heart belongs to sweet Rose. They are curious to know why and how an American can speak their language. And so, I explain to them that my parents speak French to me because their parents spoke French to them in Canada, and that Canada was once known as *la Nouvelle France*. They then understand the bigger picture, and some of the stereotypes are dropped. Most of the locals categorize Americans as either Cowboys or Indians, and so I'm supposed to be a Cowboy . . . They are not aware of how much Indian blood flows in my veins!

Another year is about to come to a close, and I have certainly seen a lot in the past two months. When Company H arrived in Le Havre in late October, we were immediately whisked off to a nearby town called Harreville-les Chanteurs, a few dozen miles away from the American Expeditionary Forces' headquarters in a place called Neufchâteau, which is somewhere southeast of Paris. It was here that the Waiting ceased, and our Training began.

A letter and two postcards arrived from Salem four days after we arrived at the base—the highlight of this period of my service. The letter was dated October 4th, so it took a full month to reach me here: the word is that mail delivery is delayed because all correspondence is censored. Believe me, it was a great joy to receive news from Castle Hill: the letter was from Rose, and there was one postcard from Valère, and one from Mr. Deschenes. This brief light, and the lightness it brought, was dimmed and weighed down by the business of preparing for this 'trench warfare'. No sooner had I read Rose's sweet lines, we were all issued a steel helmet and a temporary "room". We are sheltered within the homes of the local citizens, that is, in the barns that are attached to their stone houses: we sleep in stables and haylofts, for now.

We are getting to know the French. Each day, the training we receive is conducted by the 162nd French Infantry. I have met several peers, and even had a conversation with one, named Philippe. He is a very nice fellow, with sincere eyes, and also a catholic; and believe me, he is an experienced soldier. He has already lived *three long years* of war. Needless to say, these French fighters are tired, and their morale is very low. So here we are to relieve them. Philippe says that what he misses most are warm, home-cooked meals, and his best friend, Monique. We will see each other a lot I am sure, as we have much to learn about how to help fight this war.

I have also met a young lady, a Frenchwoman named Anne who lives with her parents, Monsieur and Madame Roussange, in Harreville. She comes to find me in the evening hours, and I have a little time to speak with her. It is a nice diversion, but I am still pining for Rose. She and her family find me a curiosity, since I speak French. They are awfully nice to me and the boys.

We have had the chance to go to church from time-to-time since our arrival. I pray to the Lord every time that I will come out of this alive and will be able to return to Castle Hill. On the other hand, we have been doing a fair amount of drinking here in France. Everyone drinks: beer, champagne, wine, and liquor. We drink when we have the chance to do so, and especially on Payday. I had my first glass of beer in France not long ago with Corporal LaCombe and Stanis, and we had a great feed along with it, so it felt like a party. There was also one day with a bottle of champagne and a fine meal. These evenings lift our spirits. Sometimes the drinking causes problems, however: there have been a few fights among the soldiers after a night of boozing. And then we are reminded of the sacrilegiousness of the Drink.

On Sunday, November 11th, after church, we were all gathered to go to see General Pershing and his staff. It is *some* staff. There was, of course, a lot of 'pomp and circumstance', but there was not much said, except for gestures of thanks and appreciation expressed by the French general 'Papa' Joffre. Black Jack wants to fight as the leader of the American Army, holding his own against the pressure to work under the command of the French. He has had to hammer out his place in this undertaking.

It has been very cold here, and this causes us to suffer. We awoke on the 27th of November with snow on the ground; and the snow and the cold, and also rain have continued since then, relentlessly. Despite the discomfort, we all managed to celebrate our American holiday here in Europe. And what a menu it was! It was *some* feed: Breakfast: steak, bread, potato, and coffee. Dinner: roast beef, bread, potato, coffee. Supper: turkey, small sweet potato, cranberry sauce, and two big doughnuts. And I won't forget it! The food and festivity certainly put us all into good spirits. At 9:30 began the sporting events: the one mile dash, the half mile race, and the 100 yards race. And "between the acts" the band played our favorite song: "When the Yanks Come Marching Home". Company H won first and second places in the one mile dash. Company H played against the Machine Gun Company in the afternoon football game. The result was a tie score of three to three. But the game reminded us of home-sweet-home, and there's no place like home, after all. It was *some* game. Afterward came the Pig Race . . . and we all really laughed our heads off. Company H came through with the big win and the prize was the pig, himself. That pig never had a chance! At least Company H played a very good, strong hand in today's sports. *Amen.*

The holiday's festivities were but a brief respite from the cold and damp weather, and the ground is still covered with snow. I have found a way to make merry without the Drink: I bought a swell fiddle without strings and bridge from one of the townspeople. I fixed her up nicely, and played her for the first time in early December. And, believe me, we had a swell time in our billeted quarters. Though, the cold weather and snow continued relentlessly outside.

In France, one celebrates Christmas by staying up all night on the Eve, while eating a grand meal called *le réveillon*, and then going off to midnight mass. Us, the soldiers of Company H, we all stayed out all night drinking beer and cognac. Gee, what a time with Roland and Stanis and the boys. We did not go to church until the morning. I felt a little funny during the mass; you know, I drank. Marmar is a liquor that will make you just as drunk as a man can be. Gee whiz, what a time.

WHEN THE YANKS COME MARCHING HOME

Our hearts today are far across the ocean
God spare our boys,
At night we kneel and pray
In far off lands our troops are now in motion
Among the very bravest in the fray
For right and might must wipe out every wrong
So let us hope it won't last long.

Our hearts are beating now with palpitation
We smile and then we brush away a tear
For we have sent the flower of our nation
We're proud of every Yankee Volunteer
America was waiting for the chance to show the love
    we always had for France.

For there'll be smiles and miles of tears,
When the Yanks come marching home
There'll be tears enough you know to make a dozen
    rivers flow
Dressed in their torn and tattered suits of tan
From battle fields across the foam
Hearts will beat with joy for every boy
When the Yanks come marching home.

For there'll be smiles and miles of tears,
When the Boys come marching home
There'll be tears enough you know to make a dozen
    rivers flow
Dressed in their torn and tattered suits of tan
From battle fields across the foam
Hearts will beat with joy for every boy
When the Boys come marching home.

—*William Jerome / Seymour Furth*, 1917.

Chapter Sixteen

Epiphany

Earlier today, at mass, I knelt down before the *crèche*, and saw that the figurines of the three wise men had been added. The kings—Caspar, Melchior and Balthazar—had been placed around the stable, extending their special gifts to Mary and Joseph. I said a prayer for myself, and for the world. We have reached the edge of a precipice, and we are all falling off. The whole world is a wound in need of mending. It needs a lot of help from this Jesus that I saw before me. I continued to pray. I suppose that all we can do is pray that someday this *débâcle* will come to an end. For now, we—Henri and I—are both grateful to be on-leave from the Front.

Maman prepared an Epiphany cake, which we found waiting for us when returned home after church. Since Henri is the luckiest of us all, he *always* gets the slice with the dried kidney bean in it, and thus becomes "king" for the day. I felt that this year would be no different. We were called back into the *salon*—which we use as a dining room only on Sundays—after our *déjeuner*, to celebrate this yearly tradition. We waited several minutes for Henri, which became a quarter of an hour. He must have gone down the road, we thought, to visit with our neighbors. We would wait to cut and serve the cake until all were present, so we decided to go out to look for him before proceeding.

This became a hunt for Henri; and worry set in. We first looked in his room, of course, and then in every room of our house. We looked in the barn and among the stables and in the hay loft; we looked high and low. Our search continued down the road at Monique's house, since he often went there to spend time with her brother, David. When we saw David and his parents, we asked them if they had seen Henri. They were, themselves, just finishing up lunch. No, they had not seen him. We pooled our thoughts as to what to do next. We all knew the fields around our property were so vast, that it was of no use to go out into them to continue our search. We would just have to accept his absence, and wait.

Back in the *salon*, the Epiphany cake stood in the center of the room like a freshly unveiled statue without an audience. We avoided it until a bonafide celebration could take place.

David, also on leave from his duty with the Sixth Army, persisted in continuing the search for Henri. He knew all of Henri's favorite secret places in the meadow where they used to go and play 'scout' together for hours on end before the necessity of going off to fight. He first looked in the dale near the creek where the pollywogs would hatch every spring. Then the search continued to *la huche*—'the beehive' they called it, a little but sturdy hut made of small branches that they had built together as fourteen-year-old boys.

David stepped inside the small space and saw Henri curled up in a ball on the ground. He was crying, and his hand was clutching a Swiss pocket knife. David sat down next to him, and put his hand gently on his trembling shoulder. A moan emerged from Henri, and then he said:

"I'm *leaving*."

"Leaving?" queried David, as he gently took the pocket knife from his friend's hand.

"I'm going to Spain."

"Spain? What do you mean?" asked David.

"I'm leaving France. I will slip away without anyone knowing. I will learn Spanish, become a Spanish citizen, settle there, and work the land."

Henri, you can't go to Spain. Your family needs you. We need you here with us."

"I will be killed in the war, anyway, like your brother. And then what use will I be to anyone anymore? No. I'm leaving . . . ."

Henri turned his head away, and let out another moan. David sat with him there, watching night fall.

*   *   *

Monique and I spent the evening together, both trying to create the pre-war atmosphere of joviality that we once knew. It was no use. We knew that we would be able to enjoy only the briefest respite from our troubles, and then the march would continue. But we both spoke from our hearts, knowing that this may be the last time that we would ever have to be together.

My dear Monique will leave tomorrow to complete her training in Paris, and then she will probably immediately begin working at a hospital in or near the capital. I took her into my arms, and tried to savor this moment. Each moment feels very precious, bittersweet.

*   *   *

We awoke the next morning to a very cold day. Henri did not join us for breakfast, and we were all, once again, plagued with worry. I ascended the staircase and walked down the short hallway which led to his room. His bedroom curtains moved with the gusts that were coming in from an open window; there was a chill which filled the room's emptiness. The note that was left on his bed, written in very light pencil, read:

> *Dear Family, I regret that I must take my leave from all of you, and from France. You should know that I will find my way; I will be okay. The life that I want to lead is no longer possible here . . . . Please know that I will hold you all in my heart, wherever I am; and that I hope that, one day, I shall see you all again. With love, Adieu,—Henri.*

It was on that early January day that I put my charm, the cherished rabbit's foot which I have had since childhood, into the garbage bin. Its luck has run out on me.

Chapter Seventeen

In the Trenches, Over the Top

I lost my translation job. I thought I was wise, but I ain't. It was Colonel LaCombe who broke the news to me; he was the messenger sent by one of the lieutenants. I will lose some income, but will gain some time with my buddies: no more afternoons riding around in trucks with the higher-ups.

New Year's Day was a big party among us. We had a bottle of cognac, and so we had a couple of mighty good laughs. We spent the day dancing and 'raising hell'. That night, though, we sat by the fireplace and thought of home-sweet-home. During mass that morning the priest certainly said the Truth. It was *some* speech; I hope it comes true. What I mean is: I hope that people really do come to their senses, and take the Word of the Lord to heart, as the pastor said.

We have been training intensively—that is, 36 hours weekly—since early November, but I went into the trenches on the Front Line for the first time at Harreville-les-Chanteurs in the Noncourt Sector during the third week of January. Since then—over the past two months—we have seen many sections of the Western Front, mostly the portion northeast of Paris. When we awoke this morning, the ground was covered with snow and mud up to our knees, and it is COLD. Home must be a paradise compared to this place.

Our preliminary training was cut short at the end of January when we were asked to reinforce the depleted Corps XI of the French Sixth Army on the 'Chemin-des Dames', and so we had to prepare to leave the training sector for *real* combat, not just trench duty. We were supposed to leave on the fifth of February, but there was some delay, so we did not entrain for Soissons until the next day at three o'clock in the morning, after a nine-mile hike in the dark. On the seventh we hiked another eight kilometers from Soissons to the town Tergnier-Chauny.

My heart went into my stomach, and there it beat madly when I saw and heard a shell burst for the first time. We were there for five days, and then we moved to a cave called *Terne d'antiche* where we stayed for another five days. It was *some* cave. These caves were a surprise to all of us doughboys, and they are serving us well for the time that we are at the Aisne Ridge. The second day in these limestone caves, I joined a reconnaissance party, and here I met a boche prisoner. He was *some* German. He looked just as scared as *we* did about the situation. And during that afternoon, I was assigned to go with the French army Captain, and so I did use some of my French, once again. It was a busy day.

Everything is moving pretty fast around me. We, the soldiers, are just trying to keep the pace, and, of course, we have to follow orders. We have all given up the wish of trying to stay comfortable, as we know there is no chance of arriving at this. The cold and damp weather that seeps into one's bones is the toughest challenge. One acclimates to the noise of the shelling and the stench of the trenches pretty fast, but one never seems to get used to the raw cold. At times like this, it's hard to remember what a summer day feels like. Only on the night before we left for Chavigny did Stanis and I get to sleep in a real feather bed.

The problem was that we were all doubled up with cramps; I'm not sure why. These were *some* sports!

On the morning of the 19th, we left the cave at Tergnier behind—Amen, and we hiked about thirteen kilometers. Our stomachs completely empty, we arrived at Chavigny at ten o'clock. We were finally issued some raw bacon which I ate ravenously, like a wild beast. However, the food rations continue to be quite small. All we are able to get for dinner were a few pieces of dry bread. Since we don't have enough food, we are tired. I want to call upon the good Lord to perform that miracle of the loaves and fishes that took place on the shores of the Sea of Galilee . . . but He is not here.

And the cold continues. We are not allowed to light fires inside the hay lofts of the barns where we are lodged in villagers' homes, due to the fear of causing a fire; so we just have to find as many layers as possible to cover ourselves up both night and day. That night we slept in barracks, but at five minutes before midnight we were displaced, because we learned that the boches were planning an air raid. The Prussian and French soldiers made an attack from one o'clock in the morning to five at night. Gee, it was great to hear our big guns giving presents to the boches! Although we are supposed to be here in reserve, backing up the French, we have certainly been more than active participants in this fight. It was also on that night that we heard something about a speech that our American President gave a few days back, something about a plan with fourteen points to try to end this fight. Only time will tell, I suppose. If only he were here with us to see what the fight really looks and feels like.

I received a box from the Salem Women's Auxiliary Club on the 21st. I think that getting this package is the only positive thing that has happened to me so far in the new year. I was more than happy to get some real tobacco. And I won't forget it.

A week after our arrival here, we were able to go to church in the village, and gee, it was *some* sight. It had been shelled and burned by the boches, almost to the ground; but we were able to attend mass in what was left of the nave of the structure. This place here reminds me of the Salem Fire.

Chapter Eighteen
Cowboys and Indians

I met Philippe once more. I knew that we would see each other again, though this bit of *destin* is not lost on me! He and his compatriots of the Sixth Army have been defending this spot on the *Chemin des Dames* for over three years now, and they are both mighty tired, and running out of soldiers. They are now our instructors, once again. I think we have boosted their morale a little.

It was in this village of Chavigny, most of which is destroyed—where were billeted in the cellars and lofts of the houses for a week—that Philippe and I had some fun, amidst the misery and boredom, and despite the February cold. An old French couple was living in that basement with us, and when they learned that I was of French descent, nothing they had was too good for me. They introduced me to all of the inhabitants of the town and to the Mayor. All of the townspeople were preoccupied with something they called 'the American Indian factor'; that is, they wondered if the American Indians had landed, and what they looked like, and 'would they murder the French people if they were let loose?', and also, 'would they scalp the Germans?' I was confused, but then also amused. Then Philippe explained that in January there had been an article in the French newspapers with the headline: *"A million wild Indians were coming from America to fight the Germans."* I knew that the Frenchmen's knowledge of Indians was gained from the Wild West movies that they had seen, thus the obsession with this 'factor'.

I brought this story back to the boys of the 104th Infantry, and gee, did they have a good laugh! We all thought that this was too good of an opportunity to miss, so we schemed. On a cold Saturday, four in my company covered their faces with 'war paint', fashioned some Indian suits out of old clothes, and—with a blanket wrapped around them—paid a visit to the Mayor of Chavigny, escorted by Philippe and me, the Frenchman and the 'Cowboy' Translator. The Mayor greeted them formally and held a party in his house with the "Indians" as the guests of honor on the last Sunday of the month. All the inhabitants of the town attended the party. Whatever the "Indians" wanted was given them, for the French people had seen at the movies the massacre that ensued when the Indians went on the warpath. Philippe and I continued to act none-the-wiser throughout the evening. What a grand time it was! The boys had a feast and carted away some of the finest cognac. I say: little do they all know how much American Indian blood runs in my veins!!

* * *

This bit of joviality was cut short by our orders to man the Aisne Line. March was soon upon us, and we were all on constant alert. We hiked for three hours to Mont des Signes from Chavigny where we had been for only ten days. When woke up on the 2nd the ground was covered with snow and mud up to our knees . . . and we were so very cold . . . chilled to the bone.

We left Mont des Monkeys at seven o'clock, on the evening of the 6th and—believe me—we had quite a scare as we made our way to the front line. Shells were bursting on both sides of the roads. But, by some miracle, we made it to the front by half past eight. It was on the 9th that we had gas for the first time, and—believe me—it was some experience. GAS. I don't dare take my mask off. And on the night of the 10th there was another gas attack—chocolate gas. Some men were caught without their masks on, and the poison made them ill. That night the orders were that we expect to move tomorrow night. *Amen.*

We did not move, as expected. We are still needed here to help out the Sixth Army. It seems that the days drag on, and we live in fear for our lives. There is a saying: "Beware the Ides of March!" And so on the 15th, we were all on alert. But it was all quiet on the front that day. The action began, instead, on the *following* day: the boches fired away, and the barrage lasted a full 24 hours. So many men are carted away on stretchers.

Orders came to us on the 22nd that our division would be moved from here to the Toul Sector, which is back where we started from, in order to relieve the First Division. We left the front line on the 23rd, and we first hiked to a village called Cuffies, enduring heavy bombardments along the way. From there we entrained and then arrived at Bar-sur-Aube in short order. The Grand Hike—which took four days, traveling about twenty kilometers-a-day—began from this place to another, called Reynel.

It was during this period of movement, that we met several French *janes*—they were some chickens!: first, at the village of Rouvres-les-Vignes, and then on Palm Sunday at Wassy, and then on the third day at Meures. We certainly had a swell time, and we got wine for nothing; but we felt cheap, because we had to leave them each time. We continued on our way to St. Blin, which was supposed to be our rest camp, but here there was no-rest-for-the-weary. Orders soon came for us to complete the last stretch of our journey to the Saint Agnant front. This swell time made me think of the popular song that we hear the French sing or hum sometimes—*Quand Madelon**

Quand Madelon
par Camille Robert et Louis Bousquet

Pour le repos le plaisir du militaire
Il est là bás à deux pas de la forêt
Une maison aux murs tout couverts de lière
Aux Tourlourous c'est le nom du cabaret
La servante est jeune et gentille
Légère comme un papillon
Comme son vin son oeil petille
Nous l'appelons la Madelon
Nous en rêvous la suit nous y pensons le jour
Ce n'est que Madelon mais pour nous c'est l'amour.

CHORUS:
Quand Madelon vient nous servir à boire
Sous la tonnelle on frôle son jupon
Et chacun lui raconte une histoire
Une histoire à sa façon
La Madelon pour nous n'est pas sevère
Quand on lui prend la taille ou le menton
Elle rit c'est tout l'mal qu'elle sait faire
Madelon, Madelon, Madelon.

2:
Nous avons tous au pays une payse
Qui nous attend et que l'on épousera
Mais elle est loin, bien trop loin pour qu'on lui dise
Ce qu'on fera quand la classe rentrera
En comptant les jours on soupire
Et quand le temps nous semble long
Tout ce qu'on ne peut pas lui dire
On va le dire à Madelon
On l'embrasse dans les coins. Elle dit "veux-tu finir . . ."
On s'figure que c'est l'autre, ça nous fait bien plaisir.
Refrain.

3
Un caporal en képi de fantaisie
S'en fut trouver Madelon un beau matin
Et, fou d'amour, lui dit qu'elle était jolie
Et qu'il venait pour lui demander sa main.
La Madelon, pas bête, en somme,
Lui répondit en souriant:
Et pourquoi prendrais-je un seul homme
Quand j'aime tout un régiment ?
Tes amis vont venir. Tu n'auras pas ma main.
J'en ai bien trop besoin pour leur verser du vin.
Refrain.

****

Confusion ruled the day because of a boche gas bombardment. On Holy Thursday, our infantry was moved hastily by French trucks and motor buses to points just near the rear of the Toul Sector. The guides manning their posts did not know how to direct us. Without having received a definite order at all, the 104th took up a position on the front line, fulfilling the general order of relief. There certainly was no respect for Holy Week on the part of the Germans.

Good Friday was also Payday. As privates, we earn 25 dollars a month. I didn't get drunk, but almost. I hope that I keep it up. Instead, I went to church.

The food has been better since we arrived in this Sector: we had corn willy for breakfast, bacon for dinner, and beans for supper. We had hopes that it would be even better on Easter, but they were dashed. On that day *reveille* was at 3:30AM, and we went to a 4:00AM breakfast of beans. We loaded ourselves onto trucks, and pulled out at 9:30AM. We are on-the-move, once again, and so tired; and there was no time to attend a mass.

73

At seven o'clock that evening we arrived at Euville, and went to bed without even a bite to eat. We did not eat again until noon the next day, April Fool's Day. That evening we moved out again, and two hours later arrived at a village called Vignot were we stayed for five days.

We had orders to pack up our furnitures, once again, at four in the morning, on the 4th of April. A six-mile hike to a place called Frémeréville began not long afterward. On this day it was a pleasant surprise to receive an Easter postcard from my little brother. A seated Jesus—holding a shepherd's crook, surrounded by three sheep, with a lamb on his lap, is pictured on the front, and at the bottom are the words: 'A Blessed Easter'. Pete's sweet note reads:

> *Cher Joseph,*
> *J'ai reçu une letter de toi le 30 janvier 1918. Tu me mande si je joue encore de la mandoline. Oui. Quand tu reviendra, on jouera une tonne. Une réponse de 'oui'. —Rosario.*

> [Dear Joseph,
> I received a letter from you on January 30, 1918. You asked me if I still play the mandolin. Yes. When you come back, we will play a lot. An answer of "yes'. —Rosario.]

* * *

*<u>Madelon</u>, English translation

<u>**Verse 1:**</u>

There is a tavern way down in Brittany
Where weary soldiers take their liberty
The keeper's daughter whose name is Madelon
Pours out the wine while they laugh and "carry on"
And while the wine goes to their senses

Her sparkling glance goes to their hearts
Their admiration so intense is
Each one his tale of love imparts
She coquettes with them all
but favors none at all
And here's the way they banter ev'ry time they call:

Chorus A:

O Madelon you are the only one
O Madelon for you we'll carry on
It's so long since we have seen a miss
Won't you give us just a kiss
But Madelon she takes it all in fun
She laugh and says "You'll see it can't be done
I would like but how can I consent
When I'm true to the whole regiment"

Chorus B:

O Madelon you are the only one.
O Madelon now that the foe has gone
Let the wedding bells ring sweet and gay.
Let this be our wedding day.
O Madelon sweet maid of Normandy
Like Joan of Arc You'll always be to me
All through life for you I'll carry on.
Madelon, Madelon, Madelon.

Verse 2:
He was a fair hair'd boy from Brittany
She was a blue-eyed maid from Normandy
He said Goodbye to this pretty Madelon
He went his way with the boys who carry on
And when his noble work was ended
He said fairwell to his command
Back to his Madelon he wended

To claim her little heart and hand
With lovelight in his glance
This gallant son of France
He murmurs as she listens with her heart entranc'd.

[Chorus A and B]

Chapter Nineteen
A Letter from France

Frémeréville, April 7, 1918

Dear Parents,

I answer your kind letter that I received a few days ago, and brought me a lot of pleasure because it tells me that you are well, and because it comes from so far away. I am very well and I hope that it is also so for all of you. I assure you that we have just spent a very sad Easter day; we did not go to mass, or to church for the whole day. I really hope that next year will be happier for all of us. I was driven around in a truck for the whole day because I am the interpreter for my first lieutenant, and that accounts for the fact that I do not have a lot of free time. But take heart, because we are going to be in Salem faster than you think, and we don't hasten to laugh, I assure you.

I saw the house where Joan of Arc was born; it is very old. When we left the trenches to rest, I assure you that we took a good hot water bath because we are very dirty. The boches are about to do themselves in; this will all be over soon, take courage. We received the *Salem Courrier* and also the *News*; it does us very well to read the news from Salem, and we see that Salem does its part for the soldiers. Tell my friends to write to me. If you only knew what a pleasure it is for us to receive letters and news from our parents and friends. When we don't have any, we feel downhearted.

Me, I can only write two letters at a time: one goes, certainly, to you, and the other, you know where it goes. It takes me some time until I am able to respond to everybody. Roland and Richard are doing well, but I don't see them very often. I have recently seen the Artillery of Salem for the first time since we left Lynnfield. It gives us great pleasure to meet friends from the same town as us.

Present my warm greetings to all relatives and friends. Take courage. From your son who does not forget you,

—*Joseph*

*   *   *

Frémeréville, 7 avril, 1918

Chers Parents,

Je réponds à votre amiable lettre que j'ai reçue, il y a quelques jours, et qui m'a fait bien plaisir, parce qu'elle me dit que vous êtes bien, et qu'elle vient de si loin. Je vais très bien, et j'espère qu'il en est toujours ainsi de vous tous. Je vous assure que nous avons passé un bien triste jour de Pâques; nous ne sommes pas allés à la messe, ni a l'église de la journée. J'espère bien que l'année prochaine sera plus heureuse pour nous tous. Je me suis fait promener en truck toute la journée car je suis interprète pour mon premier lieutenant, et c'est ce qui fait que je n'ai pas grand temps. Mais, prenez courage car nous allons être à Salem plus vite que vous ne le pensez, et nous avons hâté pas pour rire, je vous assure.

J'ai vu la maison où Jeanne d'Arc est née, cela est très vieille. Lorsque nous sommes sortis des tranchées pour nous reposer, je vous assure que nous avons pris un bon bain à l'eau chaude, car nous étions

très sales. Les Boches sont à se faire fendre la gueule, cela va être bientôt fini, prenez courage. Nous recevons le Courrier de Salem et aussi des News, cela nous fait bien plaisir de lire les nouvelles de Salem, et nous voyons que Salem fait sa part pour les soldats. Dites à mes amis qu'ils m'écrivent. Si vous saviez comme cela nous fait plaisir de recevoir des lettres, des nouvelles de nos parents et de nos amis. Quand nous n'en avons pas, nous nous en retournons la façon basse.

Moi, je ne peux écrire que deux lettres à la fois: l'une va certainement à vous, l'autre, vous savez où elle va. Cela me prend du temps avant que je puisse répondre à tous. Roland et Richard vont bien, mais je ne les vois pas souvent. J'ai vu dernièrement l'artillerie de Salem pour la première fois depuis que nous sommes partis de Lynnfield. Cela fait plaisir de rencontrer des amis de la même ville que nous.

Présentez mes amitiés à tous les parents et les amis. Prenez courage. De votre fils qui ne vous oublie pas,

—Joseph.

Chapter Twenty

No Man's Land

A swell time was had by all in Frémeré-town, where we stayed for only five days. I always feel cheap, though, when we have to leave the French girls that we meet in the villages . . . We left that place on the 10th, bound for another shelled village six miles away, Apremont. The bombardments go on for hours here, and we have to continue fighting on empty stomachs. Under heavy attack since early April, our company was on-call to fight at the left wing of the Saint Agnant line. Finally, on the 12th, some men from the 103rd were sent to reinforce us here. It was cold, and there was an ongoing mix of rain and snow during that time.

On the next day, at noon, we had the order to move into the support line without anything in our bellies. I suppose, because of the relentless bombardments, it was just too difficult to transport food to us. That morning, we had syrup and bread with coffee, and our next meal was at twenty minutes past eleven at night. At that late hour the bombardment was still going on, but—with orders—we went to bed. That turned out to be a half-hour nap; for at ten minutes to midnight, we had to go up to the line again. We were engaged in small unit close combat with the boches in a tangle of earthworks, wire, and underbrush. Though they were driven back, some of our men lost their lives in this place known as *Bois Brûlé* or "burned wood'.

I would not give a penny for my life during a bombardment, and—believe me—we have endured many by now. We all want to flee, to run for our lives; but we have orders. We have orders to stand. The past two months have shown me what War really is: War is a perpetual nightmare. And the reality of War from a trench means not only that, it means: the stench of rot, and 'trench rabbits', 'cooties', filth, fatigue, fear, deafening noise, despair, disease, contamination, boredom, blood, trench foot, trench mouth, and death.

Atop dead mules and dead horses, through shell holes—great craters in the Earth, filled with water up to our knees—and in pitch black darkness, we went on foot through the woods, eight miles, back to Vignot, according to orders, on the 13th. We found the truck and we all loaded ourselves onto it, but did not move until six o'clock in the morning. Here—in this bombed-out ruin of a town—I met the Salem boys, whom I had last seen in Lynnfield. We looked at each other in disbelief that we are still alive, but at the same time it is a look of denial of our fear, a look of bravado, of *hubris*, even. In the evening, at seventeen-hundred hours, the orders were to move—yet again, and we hiked about eight kilometers to Vertiges. We thought that we were going to stay here for a while, but after only one week we had orders to pack up; and on the 20th we made a five-and-a-half-mile hike to Bois Jony. And not two days later we were sent to Vertuzey. It was here that we had to drill for two hours per day. It feels that we have been caught in the great mythological Labyrinth in this Bois Brûlé, and the boches are the Minotaur. We feel that we are caught in a web. With their 'moaning minnies', high explosive shells, and their gas shells, the Minotaur has destroyed all communications in the sector. We have lost track with the other infantry units; the American artillery liaison has been smashed, and the result is a lot of confusion. Will we be Theseus, we wonder, and come out victorious? The question stands, however: does anyone win in War? And one fact is certain: Theseus did not have to contend with G-A-S.

We got the sad news that the boches captured almost all of the 200 men of the 102nd Infantry at Seicheprey—about fourteen miles away—in the recent standoff, and that our Division mascot, Stubby, was wounded in the fighting there. Although the general outcome of all this fighting has pushed the boches back, it came with grave consequences for us doughboys.

After ten days in Vertuzey, the orders on the 2nd of May were to pack up and to begin a hike into the woods at nine in the morning, where we stayed until the 10th. We were moved once again to a place called Xivray, where there is a nearby cave in which to take shelter and rest. We had to stand ready during the whole night, and at midnight, we had coffee. It is here that we had to go through No Man's Land, the space between enemy trenches, a barren wasteland made up of destroyed vegetation, mud-soaked craters, and rotting corpses.

Here, on the front at Xivray, once in a while some of the boys went to the hospital due to gas poisoning, and that left only 28 men holding the whole line in front of the boches. We learned that it's the same all along the front: in the 103rd Regiment, the toll of the recent bombardment was a loss of 33 men, twelve wounded, and over 150 hospitalized. Later in the week, everything was quieter, but there was more GAS . . . phosgene. It looks like we will be here at Xivray and the nearby caves for a while, if we don't suffocate first.

* * *

Enemy Storm Troops Hurled Back By Impetuous Yankees Regiment Reveals Its Valor and Fighting Qualities in the Fierce Combats of Bois Brûlé.

by AMICO J. BARONE

Apremont! The name spells horror and glory for the 104th. In **April 1918**, the troops from [. . . .] Massachusetts achieved a distinction never before won by American troops in the entire history of our armed forces. So valorously did they conduct themselves in the Bois Brule, a wood close to Apremont, that the French Government decorated the colors of the regiment with the **Croix de Guerre**. It was the first time such an honor had ever come to an American unit. In addition the regimental commander and 116 other officers and men had the bronze cross with its red and green ribbon pinned on their breasts. The regimental citation read:

"For greatest fighting spirit and self-sacrifice during action of **April 10, 12 and 13, 1918**. Suffering from heavy bombardments, and attack by very strong German Forces, the regiment succeeded in preventing their dangerous advance, and with greatest energy re-conquered, at the point of bayonet, the few ruined trenches which had to be abandoned at the first onset, at the same time making prisoners."

In a general order issued a few days after the Bois Brûlé engagements, the French general Passaga declared: "During this fight the American troops gave proof not only of their splendid courage, which we know, but also of a brotherhood in arms which was absolute and ever present. With such men as these the cause of liberty is sure to triumph."

The Croix de Guerre was also given to Captain George Roberts, and the bronze frame was specially cast with the infantry tools of the day around the frame. The frame mold was broken and never reproduced, to be one of a kind. The picture is Colonel George A. Roberts, Commander of the 104th Infantry, Westfield Massachusetts.

Bois Brûlé was in La Reine [Toul] sector on the southeasterly face of the St. Mihiel salient, a rough and ragged terrain where virtually all the tactical advantage lay with the enemy. In 1914 the sector had seen violent fighting, but as the war of attrition developed, it became moderately quiet with a sort of tacit understanding between the opposing forces to permit the situation to remain unchanged. The town of Apremont, whose name will be forever linked up with the 104th Regiment, lay outside the Allied lines. In the distance, grim and desolate Mont Sec loomed up as a splendid vantage point from which the enemy could observe the American positions: difficult spot to defend.

The 26th Division took over the sector **the first of April**, the left of the line being assigned to the 104th. On the immediate left of the [. . .] Massachusetts outfit was the 10th Colonial French Division. The regiments sub sector in the Bois Brule formed an awkward, narrow salient, hard to defend. The trenches were in poor condition, there was inadequate protection against shelling, and the marshy land made trench drainage difficult. The third battalion of the 104th, under command of Capt. George A. Roberts of Springfield, MA, immediately went into the forward position. The battalion commander, noting the small salient extending out and realizing how simple it would be for the enemy to pinch in on it and make prisoners of the men holding the position, asked and received permission to straighten out the line. K Co., under the command of First Lieutenant George Hosmer of Springfield, MA, performed this operation successfully. For some unaccountable reason, the French had persisted in maintaining the small and unimportant salient and had often lost prisoners to the enemy who would come over and successfully pinch it out. During the first three of four days the outfit held the sector, it was subjected to a harassing enemy fire. On April 5 the shelling grew in intensity and for the following four days the area was severely pounded by the enemy artillery. Evidently, an action was impending and the Germans were bent on shaking the morale of the troops by the concentration of shells.

Early on the morning of the 10th, the enemy blasting became particularly severe. The huge projectiles from the German *minnewerfers* came thundering down on the positions held by the third Battalion, shattering trenches and subjecting the men to terrific punishment. Capt. Roberts sent back word that help was needed to evacuate the wounded and suggested that the bandsmen be used as stretcher bearers. The suggestion was acted upon and the valiant work these men did under fire won for several of their number decorations from the French and American Governments. As the dawn crept over Bois Brûlé on April 10, the enemy troops made their appearance on the front held by the 3rd Battalion—a hillcrest. They came on relentlessly, but that assault wave of storm troops failed to dislodge the men of [. . .] Massachusetts. It was a severe test of arms in which much technique of warfare was forgotten by the green Yanks who nevertheless battled vigorously and effectively to beat back the veteran enemy.

The artillery fire also was of great aid in stemming that first tide. Thus for the moment the 3rd Battalion had checked the attack on **the night of the 11th** despite heavy enemy shelling, the second Battalion came in to relieve the 3rd which had held the position for 10 days. On **the 12th** the enemy came over again with renewed energy. This time the French on the American's left fell back, exposing the left flank of the Yanks. But the Americans rose to this emergency and by a vigorous counter-attack, driving back remnants of enemy groups.

Gives Credit To Men: By **the 13th** the affair of Bois Brûlé was over and the 104th had conclusively demonstrated that it could withstand the attack of seasoned troops. The men had revealed courage and resourcefulness and the officers had shown real leadership under trying conditions. A day or two later Capt. Roberts was promoted to the rank of major for the splendid manner in which he had handled his battalion. An incident characteristic of his modesty occurred at that time. The divisional commander, Gen. Edwards drove up to battalion headquarters and seeing Capt. Roberts he called him over to congratulate him. Capt. Roberts said: "The credit belongs to the men of the battalion, General, not to me." The General answered: "You would say that." On April 28, the regiment was lined up at Boucq, not far from where it had demonstrated its mettle, and there General Passaga decorated the colors of the outfit and scores of men and officers with the Croix de Guerre. His voice trembling with emotion, the French officer pinned the red and green ribbons to the 104th colors, saying: "I am proud to decorate the flag of a regiment which has shown such fortitude and courage."

Capt. Roberts was among those decorated with the French cross. He was also recommended for the American Distinguished Service Cross. Later, in the Bouconville sector, he was slightly wounded and in July he was transferred to provost marshal duty in Lanon.

—*The Republican*, Springfield, MA, 1918

Chapter Twenty One

Hope

Laffaux
le 24 juin, 1918

Monique Leger
L'Hôpital Val-de-Grâce
15, rue Val-de-Grâce
75005 Paris

Chère Monique,

Je t'écris de l'hôptial de Saint Paul près de Soissons, au village de Laffaux. Il y avait du gaz en bataille à Bazoches, et j'en étais victime. Le convalescence est très lent. Cet empoisonnement touche mon cœur, et j'ai beaucoup de douleur à la poitrine, avec un essoufflement fréquent. Ce gaz produit de l'acide chlorhydrique une fois qu'elle a été prise dans les tissus des organes. Il y a aussi beaucoup de douleur à l'estomac, avec une perte d'appétit. J'ai déjà perdu tellement de poids, je ne peux vraiment pas se permettre de perdre beaucoup plus. On dit que quelques uns des symptômes ne vont pas s'atténuer. Cet hôpital, une ancienne église, est très petite—il y a seulement une vingtaine de lits, et trois médecins disponibles—mais je me trouve sous la garde des gens capables et merveilleux, pourvu que des circonstances épouvantables.

Je regarde les portraits de Saint Paul aux mûrs de pierre, et je lui prie. Il a les yeux très apaisants.

Les boches ont nous attaqués le 28 mai, au moment où nous n'étions pas bien organisés. Nous ne savions pas que les tranchées étaient déjà remplies de gaz de phosgène et de chlorine. Et je n'ai pas senti immédiatement les effets de ce gaz . . . Ce n'etait qu'après une journée que j'avais le sentiment que je ne pouvais plus. Il y avait plusieurs autres camarades qui sont tombés de ce poison et des bombardements.

Dans quelques heures, l'enemi a gagné le village, et ensuite ils sont avancés vers Paris, traversant la Marne à Château Thierry. Ils ont gagné 40 kilomètres dans seulement quelques jours. J'ai peur pour la patrie. Notre seule espérance maintanent, c'est l'armée américaine, les Doughboys, car nous sommes, tous, tellement fatigués de la guerre.

Tu travailles, en ce moment, sans doute, dans un hôpital près de Paris. J'envoie cette lettre à Val-de-Grâce avec de l'espoir qu'elle te trouve bientôt. Ça fait déjà six mois depuis que nous nous n'avons pas vu ou parlé. Tu me manques enormément. Je t'envoie mes embrasses.

Avec tout mon amour,
—Philippe.

*   *   *

Laffaux
June 24, 1918

Monique Leger
L'Hôpital Val-de-Grâce
15, rue Val-de-Grâce
75005 Paris

Dear Monique,

I am writing to you from Saint Paul Military Hospital near Soissons, in the village of Laffaux. There was gas in the trenches at Bazoches, and I was a victim of it. My convalescence is very slow. This poisoning is affecting my heart, and I have a lot of chest pain, with a shortness of breath. This gas releases hydrochloric acid once it has been taken into the organs' tissues. There is also much stomach pain, along with a loss of appetite. I have already lost so much weight; I really cannot afford to lose much more. They say that some of these symptoms will never go away. This hospital, a former church, is very small—there are only about two dozen beds, and three doctors on hand—but I have found myself in the care of some wonderful people, given the abysmal circumstances. I look up at the portraits of Saint Paul on the stone walls, and I pray to him. He has very soothing eyes.

The boches attacked us on the 28th of May, at a time when we were not very well organized. We did not know that the trenches were already filled with phosgene and chlorine gas. And I did not immediately feel the effects of this gas . . . It was not until a day later that I had the feeling that I could not go on. There were many other comrades who fell from this poison and from the bombardments.

In just a few hours, the enemy took the village, and then they advanced toward Paris, crossing the Marne at Château Thierry. They advanced 40 kilometers in only a few days. I am afraid for the country. Our only hope now is the American army, the Doughboys, for we are all so very weary of war . . .

You are working, at present, without a doubt, in a hospital near Paris. I am sending this letter off to Val de Grace with the hope that it finds you soon. It has been six months since we have seen or spoken to each other. I miss you terribly.

And I send you my kisses.

With all my love,
—*Philippe.*

Chapter Twenty Two

Fear

Gee, it was a *good* one, the barrage of early June, pulled off by the 102nd. One million dollars in-all they say it cost Uncle Sam. A prisoner was taken afterward and named "the Million Dollar Bird". Because of us doughboys, the boches did not make the advance that they had expected.

When Company F came to relieve us, 48 hours later, we went to a big cave quarry where we got to take a bath and have our clothing steam washed. But then, not a day passed and we had to go right back into the fray. On the 12th we had a barrage; our Company—the supports—had to stand to at two o'clock in the morning. My rifle belts, my pistol, everything was ready, but they did not start anything. On the 14th word came that we would be relieved by the 103rd, but the boys did not arrive until the 16th at one in the morning. *Amen*. We had a fun time once we got to Bois Jury, after an eighteen-kilometer hike. It was not until the 24th that the news came that our Division was finally relieved of our duties in the Boucq Sector.

On the 25th I had a pass for Toul, and all of us who were on-leave met at Ménil-la-Tour that evening for a night on-the-town. I think that it was the next day that we left, undetected, via a steam-gauge tramway bound for Pagny, nine miles away. But the boches made a surprise visit to us there, dropping their bombs, very late during the night of the 27th. We survived due to some kind of miracle, I guess, because we were not at all ready to fight. It was after that close call when I took a moment to pen a sign-of-life to my sweet Rose. I now live each day with the firm understanding that I may not see the next one. We have all adapted to this way of thinking: "live for today".

Orders came to move *again*, not two days later, and we entrained at the village of Foug on a Sunday morning at one o'clock; we traveled *all day*. We were engaged in a secret operation, though we were not aware of this at that time: the 26th Division was being moved back, westward, to the Marne, closer to Paris. We were called to relieve the 2nd Division, and that meant we were whisked off to a portion of the front line called the 'Pas Fini'—Unfinished—Sector. So at six o'clock on that final day of June, we could see the Eiffel Tower and some great buildings in the distance from the vantage point of our train windows. In all, we traveled over a hundred miles, and finally detrained at a small town called La Ferté at 22-hundred hours. But the day wasn't over yet; we had to hike fourteen kilometers to Meaux, a town east of Paris. And then our regiment was transported south to Orly. The boys were a little tired when we arrived there, near midnight.

* * *

Orly: it was a nice town. All the while we were there—for three days, that is—we could hear the big guns off in the distance. Here we had to carry out drills which included a little bayonet work, a 'rehearsal' for battle. Combat without the protection of trenches, wire, and dugouts was in store, we were told. This would be "open warfare", they said, with only shallow foxholes covered with brush as 'protection'.

I took the chance to send a few more letters to South Salem, as there was more free time here than when we were at the Boucq Sector: one to Ma and Pa, and another to Rose. I awoke on the morning of July 3rd forgetting, at first, that it was my 22nd birthday. There were no festivities; rather, at suppertime it was 'everybody on deck', and we were ready to move by 7:45PM. Then later that evening, we all had a swell ride in trucks. Roland and I talked for a moment about the day when we'll be back in Salem, enjoying the Penny Arcade and Skee Ball, and dancing in Professor Kenerson's hall at the Willows.

"I can just see the dance hall filled with folks. I live for the day when I hold on to Rose's hand, and we spin around the dance floor together."

"When we get back to Story Street, I will race you to the arcade!" Roland said.

Everyone in Orly was ready to celebrate the 4th, but our plans for traditional festivities were foiled by our duties. The trucks led us into the woods, somewhere not far from Orly. The plan was to sleep there overnight. *Some* plan. *Some* fourth. We went to sleep at three in the morning, but *reveille* came shortly thereafter; and we received orders to move out, once again, in the early morning of the 5th. It was during these early morning hours that I was revisited by the dream that I had had on the day that we reached France's shores: once again, my dear family members appeared to me. Ma, Pa, René, Florida, Valère, and Pete were all there. As before they were all dressed for church, so it must have been a Sunday. Around me they stood, with a look of gratitude in their eyes; and they once again uttered the words that they knew that one day, I would, eventually, lead them into a more peaceful place. Again, this vision seemed so very strange and impossible to me, given the current circumstances . . .

Our movement brought us back into region of La Ferté. We were to fight off the boches in a place called Belleau Wood, and were ordered to pack up and take our positions on the front line on the 7th at midnight. We went back to rest at 3:30 the next day. On the 8th the orders came to do patrol work—which we carried out. A Forest of Horror is what we experienced. The Marines who preceded us faced off with the boches here to defend the capital. Such an awful fight had gone on here, we could see: the trees were all shot to pieces, the foliage destroyed. Strewn everywhere, all around us, we saw the remains of their hard-won battles: pieces of equipment—both American and German artillery—including rifles and even machine guns, ammunition, and mess kits. Worst of all were the unburied bodies, including severed limbs that were found here and there and everywhere. The putrid smell of death and decay around us made the air feel heavy. This reconnaissance mission brought us to the threshold of death.

What really spooked us was what we discovered in the clearing on the other side of the woods, in front of Bouresches. We were startled to find ourselves surrounded by boches! There must have been twenty there, all dead or near dead, some sprawling on the ground, others hanging in trees or on the wires, where our shells had probably blown them. The forest would remain haunted by these lost souls, we thought.

Just as we emerged out of the shallow trenches, the boches began to shell the town. Believe me, *I was frightened to beat hell.* When we tried to pull out of the area that night, they began to blast the road we were walking on—Paris Road, it was called. The bombardment from the German artillery went on and on, relentlessly, and it came with *mustard gas.*

I sent out prayers for my life and for the lives of the boys at my side during each day of the month of July. We lost a few men on the 10th when we fulfilled orders to move up to the front line. We could not even take a moment to mourn these lost brothers, and there is barely time or safety to bury our dead. The cruelty of war is bigger than all of us, and we have to harden our hearts. Is the Lord even *listening*? I was taught that it is not for me to question Him, so even writing this feels like sacrilege. New ways of understanding God must be brought forth, otherwise our faith is simply shattered. A war cannot possibly be any more godforsaken than what we have come to witness in the Bois de Belleau.

* * *

Orders came to go over the tops on the 18th, the first day of the next fight. It was *fierce*: man-to-man combat with the bayonet. Here, we were fighting at Bouresches. The town of Torcy and the Bouresches railway station were eventually taken by our regiment along with the 103rd, without combat. It was not until we got to Hill #193 and Bouresches Wood that we encountered the boches. And they fought back, they did! We were forced all the way back to Belleau Wood.

During these hours, which seemed to stretch on for days, I stayed as close as possible to Stanis, because I felt that this was my closest connection to my family. And if this were the time for me to greet Saint Peter, then I would have someone there to escort me to the pearly Gates. When a German soldier charged directly toward me—the look of fear in his eyes, reflecting mine—I had to lunge toward him with my bayonet. It was going to be either me or him, and I had to fight for my hide. I will never forget that sound of him hitting the ground.

The next thing I knew, Roland was down. It was the gas. I was told that he had tried to 'walk it off' but was stricken with too many of the symptoms of gas poisoning: the burning eyes and throat, the strained breathing and coughing, vomiting, dry mouth and tongue, weak legs, violet red face, and blue ears and fingernails. And then he was rushed off to the field hospital as a 'casualty'. I did not get the chance to see him before he was taken away.

On the 28th, there was relief from this hellish place. The Germans were in retreat. I never thought this day would come, when we were given orders to hike back to La Ferté where we were billeted until further notice. The Marne, so inviting, offered us place in which to bathe.

Later we learned that this ordeal, which lasted eight days, meant that the Yankee Division had just made the first real advance—of seventeen kilometers—by an American division as a unit. But in my heart I left a great loss. There is no way, now, to reclaim my innocence; and though I was thrust into this maelstrom of destruction, there is no possibility of redemption for my deeds. And I felt: this war has drawn into its center the power and the pride of all the Earth.

Chapter Twenty Three
Letters from Home

Salem, MA
August 9, 1918

Dear Joseph,

You must excuse my pencil because I started with ink and my pen is so poor that I had to take pencil. I received two letters from you yesterday one was dated June 27, and the other July 2ⁿᵈ and I thank you very much for the nice golden trio picture that you send me. Every one of you looks to be in love. Ha! Ha!

As I'm writing this letter I'm having the gramophone playing and just now I'm playing a piece. The name of it is 'Hands across the Sea'. It is a lovely piece. Tell Stanis that I bought that machine 3 weeks ago it isn't a very big one but it is big enough for us.

Yesterday I went in bathing. The water was lovely. And today we had a picnic at the Forest River Park. We had some time. It is very warm these last few days. But just now it looks like rain.

Tell Roland that Josephine, my cousin, she's got a nice little baby boy . . .

Believe me, I missed my cottage in Marblehead. But cheer up, some day I'll be <u>rich</u>, and I go again for a longer vacation.

I'm glad that you and Roland are feeling fine. It is true about the two Petit fellows—both wounded again?

Tell Roland that his cousin is all right and that he is looking fine. He now looks just like a fellow that I met on my vacation to N.H. last year. And, believe me, he was more than nice to me. But now he is gone across. He is on the surgical class. And you, why you're looking splendid: it doesn't seem if there was nothing wrong with you. Zelia sends her best regards.

With love, Rose.

*PS. Here are the white wings of love.
    May they never loose a feather,
    Until your shoes and my shoes
    Are found under the bed together.*

How do you like this one?

*   *   *

*27 Hanson Street
Somersworth, NH
August 9, 1918*

Dear Cousin—

Just a few lines to let you know that I received your letter, and was more than pleased to hear from a Soldier Boy and also my Cousin. I wish that War will be over pretty soon so we can see both of us. Now I am in the best of health, and the same thing for the old family. Sunday I went down the Beach down Old Orchard. Had some time over there. Papa is going good with his business.

Last Sunday we went down Salem, Mass. to see your poor father and mother and also the rest of the family and say that they were all in health.

Now I want to thank you for your picture, believe me, I give a good look at him. Now and then I say I look at him till I must in real person. Now again thanks and don't forget when you'll have some more picture, don't forget to send me some.

I must close and say good-bye because I got a lot of letter to write to-night. It's about 11 page that I writing and I am not through yet. I have some more to write. For now, good-bye, cousin.

from Cousine Albina B.

Chapter Twenty Four

Zero Hour

Troyon Sector
September 17, 1918

Dear Mr. & Mrs. Lavoix,

We, Joseph and I, were given orders that we had to carry out on the evening of September 11ᵗʰ. I think it was a Wednesday. We were both so weary after having hiked many miles and eaten so very little, and the weather was very stormy: there were sheets of rain here. I had just come out of a field hospital on the first of the month; I had been convalescing from taking in some poison gas that the boches used on us back in July. The equipment we were carrying, our rifles and bayonets, a shovel, and our food rations all seemed heavier to me.

Our Captain relayed the information that the aim of our mission is to 'clear the heights of the Meuse', so we finished a two-day hike in an area known as the St. Mihiel Salient. We were to force out the enemy from this spot. The terrain was very difficult to navigate, as it was pitted with old trench systems and covered with tangled masses of old barbed wire. Cutting lanes through the wire to connect with the planned barrage zone, a detail of Scouts worked throughout the night. There is no life left on these pieces of land; I suppose this is what the surface of the moon must look like.

We finally positioned ourselves near a very small village called Mouilly. This is a place about fifteen miles from the famous Verdun. Then we began the preparation of the artillery in the very early morning of the 12*th*. Joseph and I worked pretty much side-by-side during this time of setting up the guns. I could see that Joseph had become thinner since when I had last worked with him in July. Then we found ourselves ready. Stanis was there with us, too. At one hundred hours our bombardment opened. It was a "buster", and there was enough return fire to make the wait increasingly straining; so that the order to go over the top was heard almost as a relief. Before we have to go, we always whisper a quiet prayer, as we also always know that we might not make it back to the trench. At five hundred hours there was another rolling and roaring barrage, and then we heard our Captain shout: "Every man up-and-out!!" Joseph ardently grabbed my hand, looked at me dearly, and said 'God bless you!'

We all made our way across ground that provided little cover, but ample obstacles in the form of dense woods and wire, all-the-while facing heavy fire of bullets from the machine guns of the German 5*th* Army. Above us we could hear our airplanes, and we felt certain that those fliers would help us in our small, but necessary, efforts. Indeed, it was all a big success on that day, because we reached our goal of capturing some of the enemy trenches by nightfall.

Alas, there was no rest for the weary, as at midnight we were given orders to continue the fight. Although we were really more exhausted than words can describe, and had had very little to eat, we resumed the attack, with the goal, this time, to capture a place called St. Maurice-sous-les-Côtes, southeast of our position, by daybreak. On the 13*th* at three hundred hours I found Joseph taking a brief respite behind a battered tree. It was still dark and that provided cover for our advancement. He nodded at me in acknowledgement and then continued on, step-by-step, his rifle in hand. There was another barrage; the sound was deafening. It subsided by six hundred hours, and then we were able to occupy one of the enemy trenches at Saint Maurice. Here is where our company took refuge and regrouped until we were given further orders. Stanis came over to me and asked me how I was doing. We were all running only on adrenaline, and needed water, at the very least. We waited a little while for our compatriots to come in from the fight. At that time we learned the great news that the boches were now in full retreat, and that our Division now occupied several villages in the area, including Saint Mihiel, the salient, but we were not yet officially relieved of our duties. Our short-term orders were to go back through the forest and fields from where we had emerged to find our fallen and wounded.

Stanis and I went back down the heights of the Meuse. There were several men down and some were not moving. I came upon a still body, one that was prone; I heard a long, slow, faint moan emerge from him. I kneeled down over my comrade to see who it was, and then tears flooded my eyes. Joseph's face had almost no color left in it. As he was bleeding out he looked into my eyes and uttered: 'I am about to die; but God will come to you, and . . . bring you back home.' While I shrieked for help from Stanis and the others, his eyes closed, and the life just went out of him right there. Joseph had taken a grenade in the abdomen. I gathered up all of his belongings—his helmut and mask, his prayer book and journals, his pack containing the sweater that you gave to him, his rifle and bayonet—and I held onto him for as long as I could. The irony that Maurice is the Patron Saint of armies and infantrymen is not lost on me.

I want to tell you all that Joseph was my dearest friend. He gave his life for me and the men in our company. We are all united in brotherhood; so a part of me has also died and cannot be recovered now. May he rest in the kind of peacefulness that he brought to the world.

The American Expeditionary Forces lost about 3,000 brave men on that day. Joseph and the others will be laid to rest in a town located about ten miles from the battlefield, and about 50 miles from the birthplace of Joan of Arc.

I send out my condolences to you and to the entire Lavoix family. In deepest sorrow and sympathy,

—Roland.

Chapter Twenty Five
Saying *Adieu*

près de Verdun
le 11 octobre, 1918

Chers Maman et Papa,

Vous devez savoir que mon cher ami, Joseph, ce jeune homme franco-américain dont j'ai fait la connaissance à Neufchâteau au mois de novembre l'année dernière, a été tué pendant les combats récents contre les boches près de Saint Mihiel. Ces nouvelles dévastatrices j'ai reçues ce matin. Je sais qu'au mois de juillet il a brièvement fêté son vingt-deuxième anniversaire avec ses copains de Massachusetts.

*Je n'avais pas vu cher Joseph depuis, par hasard, le mois de février à Chemin des Dames. C'était le moment le plus amusant depuis que j'ai commencé cette vie de soldat. Comme nous avons rigolé à ce moment-là; car pendant une brève période de congé, nous avous joué la comédie au village. Mais, maintenant, tout celà n'est qu'une **mémoire** d'une vie—une vie abrégée, perdue au nom d'honneur, mais—à vrai dire—perdue en fraternité . . . Je suis rendu malade, encore une fois, comme une telle amitié peut être effacée—juste comme ça, dans un instant.*

Nos troupes se sont regroupées après la grande attaque coopérative à Saint Mihiel, et notre bataillon était d'accompagner le Yankee Division pour la lutte à venir qui est appelée «L'Offensive Meuse-Argonne». J'étais impatient de rencontrer mon camarade américain, et partager des nouvelles avec lui et ces copains. Mais quand je les ai vus, on m'a donné ces nouvelles affreuses. L'ami de Joseph, qui s'appelle Roland, m'a donné l'adresse de ses parents à Salem. Je vais leur envoyer quelques mots de ma part.

Ce Joseph — il était tellement cher, tellement gentil, et il était aussi une personne très dévoué — catholique, comme nous. Il avait un esprit qui était ouvert au monde, même ce monde. Il était peut-être trop ouvert. Et il avait des ancêtres de la région de La Vendée, de chez nous, il m'a dit. Son esprit vivra en moi, mais sa perte est incalculable et tellement difficile à accepter . . . et certainement encore trop dûre à accepter pour ces copains et pour sa famille . . . qui, sans doute, ne le savent pas encore.

Ton fils,
— Philippe.

* * *

near Verdun
October 11, 1918

Dear Mom and Dad,

You need to know that my dear friend, Joseph, that Franco-American young man whom I befriended at Neufchâteau in November of last year, was killed in the recent fighting against the *boches* near Saint Mihiel. This devastating news I received this morning. I learned that he had briefly celebrated his 22nd birthday with his Massachusetts friends during the month of July.

I had not seen dear Joseph since, by chance, in February at Chemin des Dames. This was the most enjoyable time for me since the beginning of this life of a soldier. How we laughed together at that time; for during a brief period of leave from duty, we put on a show in the village. But, now, all of that is merely a memory of a life—an abbreviated life, lost in the name of honor, but—in truth, lost in brotherhood . . . I am rendered sick, once again, to realize that such a friendship can be erased—just like that, in an instant.

Our troops regrouped after the great cooperative attack at Saint Mihiel, and our battalion was to accompany the Yankee Division for the coming fight which is being called 'The Meuse-Argonne Offensive'. I was looking forward to meeting up with my American comrade once again, and sharing news with him and his buddies . . . But when I saw them, they gave me the awful news. Joseph's friend, named Roland, gave me the address of his parents in Salem. I am going to send them some words.

This Joseph—he was so dear, so very kind, and he was also a very devout person—catholic, like us. He had a spirit that was open to the world, even <u>this</u> world. It was, perhaps, too open. And he had ancestors from the region of La Vendée, from our home, he told me. His spirit will live on in me, but his loss is so awful to bear for me, and surely for his friend Roland, and also for his family—who, without a doubt, do not even know, as yet.

Your son,
—*Philippe.*

Chapter Twenty Six
'With Profound Regret'

Salem, Mass.
October 16, 1918

My Dear Mr. Lavoix,

I wish to extend to you the deep sympathy of the Joint Relief Committee in the great loss that you have suffered in the death of your brave son, who died in action. Hard as it is to have him die in his youth and promise so far from home and loved ones, you have the honor of having given a man to the greatest cause the world has ever known, and his name will be held in reverence by all future generations.

If I or any member of the committee can be of service to you at this time, we shall consider it a privilege to do so. Offering you again our sympathy, I am . . .

Very sincerely yours,
—*Ernest B. Bruce,*
Chairman Joint Relief Committee.

* * *

Salem, Mass.
October 16, 1918.

My dear Mr. Lavoix:

It was with profound regret that the Ladies of Co. H Auxiliary heard of the passing on of your son in France.

He will be very sorely missed indeed and you have our deepest sympathy in your bereavement.

Yours very truly,
—*Atta M. Young,*
Secretary, Co. H Auxiliary

*   *   *

State House, Boston
October 19, 1918

Dear Madam:

I sincerely regret to inform you that I am in receipt of information reporting that Private Joseph A. Lavoix has been severely wounded while serving the in the American Expeditionary Forces.

As Director of this Bureau I am instructed by His Excellency, Governor Samuel W. McCall, to express to you on behalf of the Commonwealth of Massachusetts, her deepest sympathy. The Governor is keenly aware of the great sacrifice you have made for your Country and wishes you to accept his personal condolences.

This Bureau is at your command for such assistance and information concerning matters pertaining to the Service as you may require.

Respectfully yours,
—*Charles Baxter,*
Director of the Massachusetts' Soldier's
Information Bureau.

*   *   *

Washington, D.C.
October 24, 1918.

Dear Mrs. Lavoix:

I note in the papers with very great regret that your son, Joseph A. Lavoix, one of our boys serving in France, was killed in action. I write you this letter not to intrude at this time, but to extend my sincere sympathy and express the hope that if I can be of any service to you in your misfortune you will call on me. There may be some information you desire, and I shall be glad to try to obtain it for you if it is practicable to do so.

Yours very truly,
—*John W. Weeks, U.S. Senate*

Chapter Twenty Seven
No Possible Peace

A silence, all of a sudden, descended upon us. How *heavy* was this silence in the beginning . . . heavy, like the weight of a corpse. After a few days, the heaviness of this silence lifted. And we realized that we could put down our arms. This was almost unbelievable. We were so utterly tired, damaged, and numbed from this warrior's life.

Whispers about an armistice had been heard for many days, on the heels of the October offensive; but there were still orders to continue on with the fight, until the *bitter end*. A senseless loss of life is what I witnessed all around me during these final hours. Everyone was praying that their number would not be up during these last minutes on the battlefield, especially those of us who had been here to fight for France from the beginning.

This peace that has been wrought by the generals and diplomats is a great relief, and we are joyful, but it is incomplete. I have lost so much along the way: I have lost my neighbor, Michel, and Henri, so many of my compatriots, including dear Joseph, as well as my health and my youth. Unpacific oceans of blood have flowed into the earth. Already, people have spoken of my peers as 'the lost generation'. There can be no real peace . . .

Today I received a small envelope in the mail. It is a note from Joseph's parents, containing his prayer card. It is in French, but comes from America:

> **A la Douce Mémoire de**
> **Soldat Joseph Lavoix**
> *mort au champ d'honneur, en France*
> *le 13 septembre, 1918*
> *à l'âge de 22 ans, 2 mois et 10 jours*
>
> *Il nous a aimé pendant sa vie.*
> *Ne l'oublions pas après sa mort.*
> *Ne pleurez pas, bien chers parents.*
> *Mon sort est trop heureux.*
> *J'ai touché la terre*
> *Pour m'envoler aux cieux.*
>
> *O, Bon Jésus, donne-lui le repos éternal.*
> *Doux Coeur de Jésus, soyez mon amour.*
> *Doux Coeur de Marie, soyez mon salut.*
>
> *Adieu — Au revoir, au ciel.*

I shall write to Joseph's parents, today, during the train voyage back to La Vendée. The memories that I have of time together with their son will never be lost, and I will share them with his family members. Although I will soon see my lovely Monique, I feel lost and hopeless, and full of sorrow. There have been enough traumas for several lifetimes . . .

> **To the sweet memory of**
> **Solider Joseph Lavoix**
> *Dead on the field of honor, in France*
> *September 13, 1918*
> *At the age of 22 years, 2 months and 10 days.*

He loved us during his life.
We do not forget him after his death.
Do not cry, dear parents,
My fate is too happy.
I touched the earth
To soar to the heavens.

O, good Jesus, give him eternal rest.
Gentle Heart of Jesus, be my love.
Gentle Heart of Mary, be my salvation.

Farewell, Good bye, to heaven.

Chapter Twenty Eight

From Rosario

So Far From Story Street

Brother,
Already, when you were
Fourteen and I was just three,
You held my hand and led
The way, with glee.
Gentle eyes lighted my path,
Through city and forest, at home, and at the sea . . .
I miss you, brother.

At the sea, one summer day when I was five or maybe four,
The rip tide, under toe, nearly took me to Saint Peter.
You reached out your hand to pull me to shore.
Your strength saved me from an early demise;
I could not have asked for anything more!
I miss you, brother.

At six you took me to school on the first day;
St. Joseph's School was our second home.
You helped me learn the stories from the Book and to pray,
To genuflect, and to honor the Way

Of the Lord. Reading and writing were a breeze,
Because of your patience and kind manner.
I miss you, brother.

The years were great when I was seven, and then eight.
Antics of our rabbits and birds, and cats filled the days,
And neighbors and friends gathered in yards, and stayed until late,
Enjoying cookouts, the swing, sing-a-longs, and fun times
    all-together.
It was me on the mandolin, and you on the fiddle—what fun.
We loved the Willows, the local shops, and delicious food on our
    plate.
We felt: we have it made!
I miss you, brother.

You became a Soldier when I was nine,
Had to leave us for a time,
And stay at place called Texas, at Camp Cotton, Fort Bliss.
You dug ditches, pitched tents, cleaned rifles, and marched in line.
You saw the desert, fields of cotton, some grand landscapes and
    cities fine.
Long months passed as we waited, with hope, for your safe return.
I missed you, brother.

At ten, you came back; only to leave again—to a distant land.
Of France, I know not much,
But now I can say that I wish I could have held onto your hand,
And pulled you back home, from across the sea.
I wonder what you saw and came to understand . . .
There is a piece of me that is lost forever.
I miss you, brother.

Last year we got the news that you passed away.
Our family shrunk in size and in spirit.
To lose the very heart of our existence, we could not bear it;
We knew that we had lost our way.
Where was your calming voice? Where were your words, to say
That everything would be okay?
I miss you, brother.

J. P. LaVallee

Already, Brother,
A sign has been erected in you honor,
Planted on the corner of the streets Story and Palmer.
It bears your name with a single gold star.
But a pole cannot hug me back. I miss you, brother; for you are
So far from Story Street.

from your loving brother, — *Rosario 'Pete'*
September 13, 1919

Chapter Twenty Nine
Henri Pasquier's Farewell to Arms

Santiago de Compostella
le 25 juillet, 1919

Mon cher Philippe,

Il est grand temps que je t'envoie un mot. S'il te plaît, dis à Maman et Papa que je vais bien, et que je jouis de mon service au prespytère ici. Je continue mes études théologiques, même que je suis déjà devenu pasteur. Ma petite église—au style romanesque—se trouve auprès de la célèbre cathédrale de cette ville, qui est la destination du grand Pélérinage de Saint Jacques. Le Pélérinage de Compostelle (campus stellae, 'le champ des étoiles') commence normalement à Paris ou au Puy—et à autres endroits—en France et continue à travers la partie nord de l'Espagne dans la région de la Galice. Moi, j'ai rejoint le chemin à Bordeaux à la bouche de la Garonne, après que j'ai serré la côte, passant par La Rochelle. L'entrée aux Pyrénées se trouve dans la ville d'Ostabat, et à la frontière on traverse à Saint Jean-Pied-de-Port. C'est ici où on commence à remarquer des coquilles (les pectens)—symboles du Pélérinage de Saint Jacques—pendus sur les poteaux qui marquent le chemin pour les pélérins depuis des siècles. C'est cette route que j'ai voyagé quand j'ai quitté la France l'année dernière.

La beauté du chemin est inspirante! Alors qu'au moment du voyage je fuyais, et je ne pensais pas tellement de la Nature, en réfléchissant je peux voir comment les couleurs et les formes de la belle Terre peuvent couper le souffle. Le passage sur les Pyrénées rappelle la nature pûre de l'être humain. Les couleurs du paysage du Pays Basque remplissent l'esprit avec de l'espoir et de la bonté. Le bleu du ciel et des lacs par jour, le vert intense et rempli du chlorophylle des champs, l'orange et le rouge du ciel au crépuscule, le pourpre des montagnes, et l'or de la Voie Lactée qui illumine le ciel par nuit servent à nourrir l'âme. On sent les effets des ces merveilles naturelles non seulement au moment où on les voit, mais aussi longtemps après; car ils continuent d'imprimer l'esprit et les sens pendant des jours . . . En plus, le chemin sacré est rempli de tantes de générosités, offertes surtout par les propriétaires des plusieurs auberges sur la route.

On arrive en Espagne au village de Valcarlos, continuant à Roncevalles, et puis à Pamplona; et c'est à Puente de Reina où toutes les routes qui commencent en France convergent. Astorga était mon endroit favori du chemin, parce que c'est là où j'ai vu des ruines romaines pour la première fois, et où j'ai fait la connaissance de mon premier ami espagnol, Señor Carlos Mogaburo-Cid. Carlos, né à Astorga, est le propriétaire du Refugio de los Inocentes (L'Auberge des Innocents). Il a un petit singe qui divertit les voyageurs pendant leur séjour d'une nuit. Plein de bonté, il a encouragé mes voeux de poursuivre la paix plutôt que la guerre.

La majestueuse Cathédrale de Santiago vous accueillit après plusieurs journées de marche. Je suis entré là-dedans pour voir le tombeau de Saint Jacques-le-Majeur—l'un des apôtres de Jésus, un missionnaire, et le Patron des Travailleurs et des Pèlerins—et j'ai vu les vaisseaux qui contiennent ses reliques. Tants de pélérins ont mis la main sur le pilier juste à l'intérieur de la porte de l'église, qu'une rainure a été creusé dans la pierre.

Ayant voyagé plus de mille kilomètres à pied, je suis allé directement à la mer d'une manière traditionnelle pour obtenir mon propre souvenir du voyage—une coquille de pectens, nommée 'la coquille Saint Jacques'.

Celle-ci est l'épreuve qu'on a été au bout de son chemin. On la porte à la poitrine, et puis on sait que vous êtes un vrai Pélérin.

Chaque jour j'adopte—de plus en plus—les moeurs des espagnols. Leur sagesse collective dépasse celle de nous, les français; surtout parce qu'ils ne se sont pas mêlés de la guerre. Les espagnoles sont plus indépendants d'esprit que d'autres au Continent, et beaucoup parmi eux conservent encore l'idéal de la création d'une utopie. Et tandis que je pense que l'Espagne est à peine une utopie aujourd'hui, la vie ici est beaucoup mieux que celle que j'ai temoignée et connue en France.

Je lis, en ce moment les œuvres inspirants d'André Gide, notre contemporain. Il nous dit: "Il est plus facile de conduire les hommes au combat, en remuant leur passion, que de les retenir et de les diriger vers les travaux patients de la paix."

Je t'embrasse très fort. Que Dieu te bénisse,
—Henri

*   *   *

Santiago de Compostella
July 25, 1919

My dear Philippe,

It is high time that I send word to you and family. Please tell Mama and Papa that I am well, and enjoying my service in the parsonage here. I continue with my theological studies even though I have already become a pastor. My little church—created in the Romanesque style—is located adjacent to the famous cathedral of this city, which is—of course—the destination of the great Pilgrimage of Saint James. The Pilgrimage of Compostella (*campus stellae*—'the field of stars') normally begins in France in Paris and Puy—as well as other places—and continues across the northern part of Spain, known as Galicia. I joined the route at Bordeaux, at the mouth of the Garonne, after hugging the coast, passing through La Rochelle. The entrance into the passage over

the Pyrenees begins in the town of Orthez, and at the border
one passes at Saint Jean-Pied-de-Port. It is here that one begins
to notice scallop shells (*pecten conchis*)—the symbol of the
Pilgrimage of Saint James—that are placed on posts. These have
marked the route for pilgrims for centuries. This is the route that
I traveled when I left France last year.

The beauty of the route is inspiring! While at the time of
the voyage I was fleeing, and not thinking so much about
Nature, in retrospect I can see how the colors and forms of the
beautiful Earth can take one's breath away. The passage over the
Pyrenees brings to mind the pure nature of human beings; the
landscape of the Basque Country fills the mind with hope and
goodness. The blue of the sky and the tarns by day, the intense,
chlorophyll-filled green of the fields, the orange and red of the
sky at dusk, the purple of the mountains, and the gold of the
Milky Way that illuminates the sky at night all serve to nourish
the soul. One feels the effects of these natural wonders not only
at the time of seeing them, but also for a long while afterward; for
they continue to impress upon the mind and the senses for days.
In addition, the sacred route is filled with so many generosities,
offered, especially, from the proprietors of the many hostels
along the way.

One arrives in Spain the in village of Valcarlos, and a little
while later, one comes upon the towns of Roncevalles and
Pamplona; and it is at Puente de Reina where all of the routes
that begin in France converge. Astorga was my favorite place
on the route because it was there that I saw Roman ruins for the
first time and where I met my first Spanish friend, Mr. Carlos
Mogaburo-Cid. Carlos, born in Astorga, is the owner of the
Refugio de los Inocentes (Hostel of the Innocents). He has a pet
monkey which entertains the travelers during their overnight
stay. Full of goodness, he encouraged my wishes to pursue peace
instead of war.

The majestic cathedral of Santiago greets you after many
days of walking. I entered inside to view the shrine of Saint

James the Greater—one of the apostles of Jesus, a missionary, and the Patron of Laborers and Pilgrims—and saw the vessels that contain his relics. So many pilgrims have laid their hands on the pillar just inside the doorway of the church that a groove has been worn into the stone.

Having traveled over a thousand kilometers on foot, I finished off the journey in the traditional fashion with a final walk to the ocean to get my very own souvenir of the voyage—a scallop shell, named the 'Shell of Saint James'. This is the proof that one has reached the end of the Way. One wears it on the chest, and that way others know that you are a true Pilgrim.

Each day I adopt, more and more, of the ways of the Spanish. I feel that their collective wisdom surpasses ours, mostly because they kept themselves out of the War. They are more independent-minded than those on other parts of the Continent, and many among them still preserve the ideal of creating a utopia. And while I feel that Spain is hardly a utopia today, life here is far better than what I have witnessed and experienced in France.

I am reading the inspiring works of André Gide, our contemporary; do you know of him? He tells us: "It is easier to lead men to combat, stirring up their passion, than to restrain them and direct them toward the patient labors of peace."

Sending warmest wishes. May God bless you,
—*Henri.*

Chapter Thirty
Gold Star Mother

My Son

God gave me my son in trust to me;
Christ died for him, and he should be
A man for Christ. He is his own,
And God's and man's not mine alone.
He was not mine to "give". He gave
Himself that he might help to save
All that a Christian should revere,
All that enlightened men hold dear.

"To feed the guns?" O torpid soul!
Awake and see life as a whole.
When freedom, honor, justice, right,
Were threatened by the despot's might
With heart aflame and soul aright,
He bravely went for God to fight
Against base savages, whose pride
The laws of God and man defied;
Who slew the mother with her child
Who maidens pure and sweet defiled.

He did not go "to feed the guns,"
He went to save from ruthless Huns
His home and country, and to be
A guardian of democracy.

"What if he does not come?" you say;
Ah well! My sky would be more gray
But thru clouds and the sun would shine,
And vital memories be mine.
God's test of manhood is, I know,
Not "Will he come?" but "Did he go?"
My son well knew that he might die,
And yet he went with a purpose high,
To fight for peace, and overthrow
The plans of Christ's restless foe,
He dreaded not the battle-field;
He went to make fierce vandals yield.

If he comes not again to me
I shall be sad; but not that he
Went like a man—a hero true—
His part, unselfishly, to do.
My heart will feel exultant pride
That for humanity he died.

"Forgotten grave?" This selfish plea
Awakes no deep response in me
For, though his grave I may not see,
My boy will ne'er forgotten be.
My real son can never die;
'Tis but his body that may lie
In foreign land, and I shall keep
Remembrance fond, forever deep
Within my heart for my true son,
Because of triumphs that he won.
It matters not where anyone
May lie and sleep when work is done.

It matters not where some men live;
If my dear son his life must give,
Hosannas I will sing for him,
E'en though my eyes with tears be dim.
And when the war is over, when
His gallant comrades come again,
I'll cheer them as they're marching by
Rejoicing that they did not die.
And when his vacant place I see
My heart will bound with joy that
He was mine so long—my fair young son
And cheer for him whose work is done.

—*Dr. James L Hughes*
[of Toronto, in reply to Edwin Markham's propaganda
verses: "I Did Not Raise My Boy to be a Soldier."]

My Star

I wear a gold star on my breast,
A star of strife, a star of rest;
It marks a sword thrust through my heart,
It tells of glory and of pain,
Of bitter loss and wondrous gain,
Of Youth that played the hero's part.

O star of gold upon my breast,
Tell of ideals that he loved best;
He braved the foe, he suffered all
To keep our banner free from stain,
He hath not given all in vain
In answering his nation's call.

O star of hope upon my breast,
Strengthen the faith I have professed,
He died that nations might be free;
Help me to live for truth and right,
And with a stalwart soul to fight,
Nerved by his immortality.

—Catherine Ticknor,
Boston Transcript

Salem News, June 17, 1930
Local Gold Star Mother to Sail Abroad, June 25th.
Mrs. Lavoix Receives Notice from Government; to Visit Battlefields; Will Be Accompanied by Friend.

Mrs. Placide Lavoix, 38 Story Street, mother of **Joseph A. Lavoix** *of this city, who was killed in action in France, Sept. 13, 1918, received notice from the government yesterday, to sail from New York on June 25th with other gold star mothers on a pilgrimage to the battlefields arranged for by the war department.*

Although the gold star mothers of Massachusetts were allotted 23rd place in the drawing of the states for positions, the local woman was able to get into one of the early quotas by a request she made. Otherwise, she would not be making the trip until the latter part of 1931 or early 1932 when others from this state will make their sailings.

Accompanying the Salem woman will be Mrs. Amelia Valcourt, 15 Nesmith Street, Lawrence. Mrs. Lavoix read in newspapers that the Lawrence woman was to make the trip, and as she preferred to make the pilgrimage with another French person, arrangements were completed to have her sail with the Lawrence gold star mother.

The first of the gold star mothers are sailing on May 7 of this year and it will be 1932 before all of them have set sail to view the final resting spots of their sons in the battlefields. The plans for the trip have been worked out so well that each mother will be able to tell in advance, almost to the hour, how and where her time will be spent on the entire trip. All arrangements were made by the government. Transportation and expense money from their respective homes to the port of sailing will be provided in advance. On arrival in France they will be met by army officers and escorted to first class hotels. Their first day will be one of rest in Paris. Trips to the tomb of the Unknown Soldier, receptions by government officials, trips to cemeteries and battlefields will then follow.

Over There

In a line, a procession of black, the widows and mothers came off of the ship at port in Cherbourg. Wearing a long black skirt with a matching blazer, a gray blouse, black hat, and black shoes, Joseph's mother emerged from the group. I recognized the very kind, but worn, look on her face, since she had sent along a photograph of herself a year ago. Her smile and the light in her eyes were dimmed by so much sorrow. She was surprised to see us there, for she had not yet received my letter. We had enough time to lunch together in the town before she had to rejoin her group and board the train bound for Paris.

Mrs. Lavoix looked at me with a half smile; and though she was subdued, I could sense that she was very touched by our presence—which, of course, could not completely assuage her grief. It was wonderful for us—Monique, little Christophe and me—that we were able to converse, since she speaks a fluent French, though with a strong Canadian accent that was sometimes hard to decipher. I told her about how I met her son during the training period in Neufchâteau, of the fun we had in the village of Chavigny, and also of the awful days when our endurance was stretched to maximum levels, and when we were on the threshold of death at the Chemin des Dames front. She asked many questions, but she was not of the mind to share with me stories of Joseph's childhood, of their life together in Salem. No, she could not be moved out of her solemnity. I think that the loss of a child is probably the worst pain that one can suffer, and I understand this so much more now that Christophe is among us. Well, I know now that she has lost *seven*; for I learned, via letter, that Joseph's younger brother died three years ago. Valère was struck by a lung infection, and the sulfur did not work to stop the pneumonia. Like his elder brother, he was just 22. Three children now remain out of the *ten* that she brought into the world. I would say that this is enough grief for several lifetimes.

A devout woman, Mrs. Lavoix shared with us that, frankly, her faith is tested. She wonders why she has had so much to bear; but that she does not dwell on the question too long, or else she would be utterly inundated by grief. She said that she has to remain strong for her other children—a daughter and two sons—who are now in their twenties, and trying to find their way in the world. But, as far as I can see, it has been as if a great shadow has been cast over the Lavoix family, and how long that shadow may extend on into the future, only time can tell . . . Some may even call it a *curse*, the kind of which one reads about in a Greek tragedy. The forlorn look on her face may never be erased.

Our lunch was abbreviated by the request that Mrs. Lavoix meet up with her group at the Gare de Cherbourg. The Paris-bound train would depart soon, and then the women were to follow a detailed itinerary has been mapped out for their two-week sojourn, this pilgrimage to their sons' or husbands' final resting places. I bid Joseph's mother *adieu*, with the hope that we would be able to meet again in Paris in a fortnight, before her return to America.

* * *

Afterword: The 'Necklace'

Despite the immeasurable pain and deep wounds caused to my ancestors because of service in both of the World Wars, my father was a Patriot. Before he was even graduated from high school, he tried to enlist in the Marine Corps. They sent him out of the door, telling him to return when he was eighteen. Soon after coming of age, he joined the US Air Force, and served for four years and reenlisted for a fifth. He desperately wanted to go to Vietnam in the early 60s, but my birth blocked his way; that is, one could not be drafted to go if one had more than one dependent. I was the second born. Despite the loss of my great uncle, and despite the years of youth taken away from at least two other of my father's uncles who served in World War II, my father brought me to the campus of West Point Military Academy at the age of fifteen so that I could have a look around. He gave me a nickel-plated pistol for my sixteenth birthday, for he wanted me to become a Markswoman. Much to my father's dismay, I chose the liberal arts campus of Wesleyan University instead. The honor and the glory that he associated with military service eluded me. After all, my generation, who grew up in the anti-war climate of the 1970s, had been weaned on the soundtrack of the Broadway musical "Hair": when I was five years old, in 1969, my best friend and I spent hours drawing and painting multi-colored 'Peace' and 'Love' signs, and posting them 'everywhere'.

Although my father never met his Uncle Arthur—his own father was only eleven years old when Arthur was killed in France—his memory lived on in my father's heart and mind. I remember him telling us that he had to write yet another letter to the Salem municipalities to remind them to resurrect the "LaVallee Square" sign and signpost at the corner of Palmer and Congress Streets that was planted there in Arthur's memory. I remember seeing it when I was a small child: the gold letters "Pvt. Arthur G. LaVallee" and a gold star were painted onto a black background. All of the young men of Salem who lost their lives in France were memorialized in their neighborhoods with such a sign. The new inhabitants of South Salem in the 1970s—those who moved in after the French-Canadians had migrated out—repeatedly pulled it down. On at least two occasions my father wrote letters to the *Salem Evening News* to inform them of the vandalism to public property. Today, there is no trace of it.

So who was this War Hero, I wondered? I knew, at least, that his story meant something to my father. Later in my life I would learn more about him. But before I realized that I would write his story, I was already collecting experiences that would add to my understanding of his life and times. Looking back on them, I have come to understand that I am *meant* to write it. There was a calling to this task. It is as if, when one is born, there is a pearl necklace that one needs to string up; though one has to take the time to find each-and-every pearl, and then to assemble them on one's own. This story, based on the abbreviated life of Arthur, is my 'necklace'.

I would say that the first 'pearl' came to me as a toddler. My father's great aunt, Aunt Rose, still lived at number 12 Story Street, one house down from her childhood home, and we lived next door to her at number 14, the last house on the street, which her father had built. This Salem neighborhood was known to its denizens as 'Castle Hill'. Aunt Rose was in her late seventies at that time, and she crossed the yard to our porch, gifts in hand. She gave each of us, my sister and me, a small woolen blanket for our dolls. It has a pattern of light and dark blue checks, and the edges were finished by her using the blanket stitch with yellow yarn. I have kept it safe to this day. I remember a story about Aunt Rose: she wore a black wig her whole life because of a factory accident that occurred when she was only sixteen. Her long hair got stuck in one of the mechanical looms at the textile mill, and she was 'scalped' by the machine. There were many such 'factory accidents' at the time, which I would learn later when studying the Industrial Revolution. The fabric that she gave us that day may have been manufactured by the looms upon which she had worked.

At the age of four our family moved to my mother's hometown; my father bought a house on Farley Avenue in Ipswich. Later in life I was to learn that our street was named after Captain Theodore Rogers Farley, a veteran of both the Mexican border campaign and of WWI, just like my great uncle. He would likely have met Arthur in November of 1918 during the last three days of the war if Arthur had not been killed. A short biography of him reads: *Theodore Rogers Farley: born at Ipswich, November 22, 1894. Son of George E. and Emeline F. Farley. Married Miss Gladys St. Clair at Buffalo, NY, August 4, 1917. He enlisted June 18, 1916, in Buffalo, in the 65th Infantry, New York State Guards, and was stationed at Camp Whitman, NY. On July 12 he was transferred to the 3rd Field Artillery, and had been promoted to Sergeant when the regiment was sent to the Mexican border in September. Having passed a successful examination at Brownsville, TX, Jan 23, 1917, he was commissioned 2nd Lieutenant January 23, 1917, and was then the youngest commissioned officer in the National Guard. He was commissioned 1st Lieutenant October 1st, 1917, at Spartanburg, SC, were he remained until called for service in the War of the Allies. He was assigned to the 106th Field Artillery, went overseas in the Matsonia, landing at St. Nazaire. After a short period in a training camp in Bordeaux his regiment went to the Verdun Sector. On September 11th at 11:59, zero hour, his battery joined in the heavy fire that opened the St. Mihiel drive and advanced with the infantry, stationed about a mile in the rear of their line. Then it was ordered to Montfaucon, where it suffered many casualties, and at Gercourt pressed the enemy so hard that three batteries of German guns, with their sights in place and their ammunition, were captured and turned upon the retreating foe. Lieutenant Farley was lightly gassed in the sharp fighting in the Argonne Forest, but was not disabled, and was with his battery in action on the west and east banks of the Meuse. The last three days before the armistice on November 11th, his guns supported the 104th Infantry, in which were a number of Ipswich boys. On October 20, 1918, he was promoted to the rank of Captain on the field of battle, in the face of the enemy, but had been in virtual command of his company since June, 1918. Discharged May 21, 1920.*

The next 'pearl' came along several years later at age thirteen. As an eighth-grader, I was selected to read a poem to the assembled school community on Memorial Day at the Whipple Junior High School in Ipswich, MA. The Principal made the selection—of both student and poem. With butterflies in the stomach, I read: 'In Flanders Fields' by Lieutenant Colonel John McCrae of Canada, before an audience of about 300 people. This poem is the literary symbol of World War I.

At fifteen years old I went to France. My high school French Teacher organized a two-week exchange program, and I eagerly took part. We landed at Charles de Gaulle Airport on April 13, 1979. The very next day, my host family decided to take a four-day holiday during the Easter weekend. All of the other American students spent these first days touring Paris, but I went on a very unusual road trip. This was the third 'pearl'.

We began our excursion early in the morning, bound for Verdun. My exchange student's father wanted to show me the WWI memorials there, including the Lighthouse and Ossuary of *Douaumont*, and what was left of the Trench of Bayonets—a great scar in the earth. I took several photographs with my father's small Kodak camera, though I felt that I was simply a tourist with, as yet, no emotional connection to the place. We then continued on our way to Alsace through Strasbourg, and then on the second day we crossed the border into Germany. I was yet not aware that it was this territory that had been the 'bone of contention' between France and Germany for centuries. Going south, through the Black Forest, we stopped the lake town of Titisee, where we spent the night. I remember seeing a rainbow over the lake while we enjoyed riding in the paddle boats—a good omen, and symbol of a bridge from one world to another. On the following day we dipped into Switzerland, at Rheinfall. We returned to their home in Bondy, in the suburbs of Paris, on the 17th. Of course, I was not aware what an important trip this was to be for me.

The Author (R) and her French exchange student in Verdun, at Lighthouse of Douamont, April, 1979.

I continued studying French after high school at Wesleyan University. I suppose that it was no accident that during my sophomore year there I crossed paths with Sebastian Junger who was in his junior year. We sat in two of the same classes together: French Literature and Sociology, and we began an acquaintanceship that continues today from the distance of life's divergent paths and extenuating circumstances. I thank Sebastian, author of *War*, and Co-Director of the Emmy-winning film documentary, *Restrepo*—among other acclaimed works, for offering his support and encouragement of this work. One could say that our meeting was the next 'pearl'.

When I was 22 years old it was my father's idea that we go to France together for two weeks, as a graduation present. This offer surprised me because I knew that he was very upset by the fact that I had chosen to attend a liberal arts college over the military academy. My father simply wanted to see France; there was no set agenda. We would stay in Paris for a few days, and we would also rent a car and drive around a bit. Once we got to Paris and settled into our hotel on Rue de Rennes, we both thought that it would be a good idea to try to find where his Uncle Arthur was buried in Saint Mihiel. At the time, I was not familiar with the details of my great uncle's death; but my father, on the other hand, had grown up with the stories. He knew that Arthur had been killed during the Battle of Saint Mihiel in September of 1918, and that Saint Mihiel was near Verdun; so for the second time, I got into a car, and drove to that area, about 165 miles east of Paris. This was, of course, pearl number five.

I was the very same age that Arthur was when he died there. We arrived in Saint Mihiel, and there we learned of a Memorial for American Soldiers in WWI at Montsec. When we got there, we discovered that it was not a burial ground, but a rather large, white monument in the style of a Greek Temple. We began asking others about the location of an American cemetery, and learned that, indeed, there was such a cemetery not far away in a town called Thiaucourt, about ten miles away. We zigzagged through the village roads until we finally came upon the place.

We signed the Register, but we realized that we were on our own to search for Arthur's headstone among the more than 4,000 marble crosses. My father started out on the left-hand section, scanning three rows at a time, while I looked on the right side. Minutes later I found it: Arthur's grave. There lay his remains. It was an emotional moment. We took some photographs. I was glad that my father was able to see this spot; and he was also very moved.

My father at Arthur's gravesite in Thiaucourt, August, 1985.

A few years later, I moved to Cambridge, Massachusetts. It was here that I continued teaching French, and it was then that I began writing. During the fall of 1990, I made a trip to South Salem to take pictures of my father's old neighborhood. The area, now known as 'the Point', had, sadly, become very run down. The French Canadian population began an exodus in the late 1960s, and the new immigrant population moved in and had established themselves there by the mid-1970s. My grandmother was the last of the family members to move out of this area in 1973 or so—an area which is now still considered a kind of 'no man's land'. Every time my father passed through his old neighborhood he became distraught. There was a lot of nostalgia about the place. During my October visit—an excursion which turned out to be the sixth "pearl"—I took many photographs to document the vestiges of what had once been a thriving section of the city. It seemed so barren, so hollowed-out. I found the house I lived in at birth—on the same street where Arthur had lived—and continued to snap pictures of places that my ancestors built and frequented, including my grandfather's barber shop, and tried to feel their presence there. I remembered my own footsteps there as a toddler. The result of this series of photographs, taken on that day, is the cover illustration of this book.

Almost two decades passed until the lucky seventh "pearl" surfaced. In the meantime, life had brought me to work, study, and write in Cologne and in New York City. During an afternoon visit with my father at his home in Ipswich, MA, he pulled out a long, slim cardboard box from his desk drawer, and handed it to me saying: "Jeanne, I think you may want to have this." It was an 'Everyman's' hosiery box, and quite old. I opened it to find a 'treasure': several very small notebooks which were turned into diaries, penned by his great Uncle Arthur during his life as a soldier. In addition, there were several postcards, letters and photographs, all collected there, documenting Arthur's last years of life. I took them with the idea to read and transcribe the journals so that my father and his favorite uncle could, finally, read their contents. I made copies of everything for myself. This box had been housed in my father's desk drawer, untouched, for over thirty years. His father, Arthur's brother, had surely passed it to on to him. Upon reflection, it was as if two generations wanted to keep all the pain locked up inside this 'Pandora's' box. It has taken, I suppose, almost one hundred years to find the proper 'key' to unlock this box, and uncover the source of two generations of suffering . . . This pain is still being processed.

I had always thought about writing about the French-Canadian experience in New England as part of a personal memoir. I even collected some books on the topic, several of which I found at the book shop of the National Historical Landmark, which an entire district of Lowell, MA is now designated. I also conducted an oral history of my great aunt and uncle before moving to Germany. The feeling became stronger when I realized that I had lived on "Story" Street—there was a story to be written. And what astounded me later was realizing that the streets that run parallel along Jefferson Avenue are, respectively: Read Street, Arthur Street, and Wilson Street . . .

In July of 2010, my father passed away at the age of 71. It was then that I felt that an era had passed. The following year, I read Julia Cameron's wonderful book "The Artist's Way"—the eighth 'pearl' along the Way—and began implementing one of the recommended exercises into daily activities: The Morning Pages. It was in writing these daily pages that I discovered that voice inside of me, 'calling' me to write Arthur's story. That's when I began, in earnest, putting it to the page.

Joseph Campbell, in the "Power of Myth" interviews with Bill Moyers, said: "Looking back over one's life, there seems to be an order to things." I have found this to be so in my life. I can perceive an order in what seemed to be chaos at the time.

Germany and German Friends

Upon reading Rainer Marie Remarque's very moving book, *All Quiet on the Western Front,* one can see that the Great War benefitted noone, least of all the German peoples, themselves. I have had the good fortune of visiting Germany several times, and had lived there for a total of about two years. During these sojourns I have come to know so many wonderful people, including: the Curic family, the Gaspers and König families, the Schneider, Arz, and Anders families, the Zimmers, Frau Anneliese Kewenig and the von Andreae family, the Fay-Gerner-Beuerle family, Susanne Hoeke, Dr. Jantje Roeller, Prof. Dr. Anslem Haverkamp, and many others, both from my travels, and from my studies at New York University. Each encounter has enriched my life. In addition, I spent fifteen years researching and writing about the life and work of the German Sanskrit Scholar and first Comparative Mythologist, Heinrich Robert Zimmer, who was Joseph Campbell's mentor in the early 1940s.

German Culture—including, Painting, Literature, Music and Architecture—has enriched my life. I have also enjoyed the beautiful landscapes of many regions of Germany, including the hills of the Eifel, many lakes of Bavaria, and the great Rhein River during my many visits and stays. It is a great tragedy for all on the Continent—the French and German peoples alike, that they had to suffer such chaos and hardship during the twentieth century due to decisions made by a handful of people—by 'the one percent'.

Arthur's Journals

I am the lucky recipient of young Arthur's journals and personal papers that were preserved inside my father's desk drawer for over 30 years; and they were surely kept safely in my great grandfather's care, and then my grandfather's, for a total of three generations. And I will, in turn, give them to my daughter. The slender green cardboard box contains: family photographs, postcards from El Paso, TX, correspondence from the US government and from friends and family, a Catholic prayer book, as well as four small booklets, three of which served as Arthur's diaries during his two campaigns. Ironically, upon one of the blood-stained books that Arthur would have used as a diary, it is written 'New England Mutual', and on the inside of the black leather cover there are more details: 'New England Mutual Life Insurance Company', Boston, MA. The first set of Arthur's journal entries span from June 19 to November 6, 1916; and the second set of entries run from July 25, 1917 to July 28, 1918. From March 30th to July 18th he made entries in a third journal. After having experienced the gas of trench warfare, Arthur's handwriting becomes smaller and smaller. The final three entries read:

> *July 10, We went to the front line. There we lost a few men.*
> *July 18, Orders came to go over the tops. It was fierce. July*
> *28, Relief. We hike to . . .*

In the journal which was abandoned on March 9th, there is another entry for July 18th which reads:

> *At 6 o'clock orders came to get ready to go over the top at 8*
> *o'clock. The boches were shelling our place to beat hell.*

Amidst the chaos of what the young men had to endure on a daily basis, it is no surprise that there is some confusion with the journal entries made in France.

Since French was my great uncle's first language—as well as my parents' first language—many of the entries, especially in the first journal, are written in French. I have made translations wherever necessary for the purposes of the narrative.

After reading through and transcribing these documents, I shared them with both my father—who had never read them—and his Uncle Frank. Frank, (Francis Tardiff, 1912-2008) served for three years in WWII, was almost killed in action on at least two occasions, and earned the Purple Heart for his efforts.

When he was 93, I asked him if he had met Arthur as a young man. Yes, he said he had. Frank was five years old when Arthur was sent to France, but he remembers that Arthur went off very reluctantly. NB: As a soldier, Frank had walked the entire length of the country of Italy, and had been embroiled in many battles. On one occasion, he witnessed his best friend die before his eyes: just next to him, a shell burst, tearing of his friend's legs from the torso. He bled to death more quickly than Frank had time to react. The shells continued to fire all around them while Frank watched, in shock. Frank, himself, took some shrapnel in the head, and it was simply some sort of miracle that he survived without any permanent damage to his skull or brain. Frank said that he had a really nice connection with the surgeon who pulled out pieces of debris from his head at a hospital in New York City. In addition, Uncle Frank was two years old when the conflagration of Salem engulfed two thirds of the city. He remembered his father, he told me, telling him to hold a hose onto to roof of their house in preparation for the blaze; but the fire did not reach their home in Castle Hill.

The contents of the hosiery box and the transcriptions sat idle for another five years before beginning this work. In many instances I have copied Arthur's journal entries verbatim and inserted them into the narrative. Also, all of the letters contained in the box—including ones from Arthur, Rose, my grandfather, Arthur's first cousin, Albina Boulanger, and the government agencies—are included with only minor alterations.

It is a great gift that Arthur's journals have been preserved for nearly a century. They are now historical documents. Those who have original letters, diaries and other documents are encouraged to submit copies to:

The Legacy Project
P.O. Box 53250
Washington, DC 20009

Arthur in uniform with a friend in Salem, circa 1916.

Chere Parents—

Je vous envoie quelque vue du fameux mexico. C'est ici que vous voyons des (Gringo) Mexicum. On est a seulememt 50 verge du border. Il nous regarde et ou les regarde j'ai hate d'aller au devant d'eux autres. je voudrais leus si belle moustache. Albert et moi nous somme ensemble encoure une fais.

De votre Fils
Arthur.

Note from Arthur to his parents from El Paso, TX.

Arthur on horseback in Salem, circa 1917.

From right, Placide and Celanire (Arthur's parents)
and friends on porch, Salem, MA.

Arthur's blood-stained prayer book

Soldat ARTHUR LAVALLEE

mort au champ d'honneur, en France

le 13 Septembre, 1918

a l'age de 22 ans, 2 mois et 10 jours

Il nous a aimé pendant sa vie
Ne l'oublions pas après sa mort
Ne pleurez pas, bien chers parents
Mon sort est trop heureux
J'ai touché la terre
Pour m'envoler aux cieux

O Bon Jésus donnez-lui le repos eter-
nel—7 ans et 7 quar-d'ind.

Doux coeur de Jésus soyez mon a-
mour
Doux coeur de Marie soyez mon
salut—300 Jours d'ind chaque fois

Adieu—Au revoir au ciel

Prayer Card, upon Arthur's death.

Celanire LaVallee (Gold Star Mother) in France circa 1930.

Afterward

Looking back, one can see that the pain of the loss of Arthur had the effect of a plague upon the LaVallee family. At the time of Arthur's death, his remaining siblings are ages eleven, thirteen, sixteen and eighteen. The family had already suffered the loss of five children either during birth or due to the common childhood diseases of the time, of pertussis and diphtheria: Célanire, Arthur Joseph, Eva Gracie, Elida Marie, and Noel Alfred. In 1927, Valère dies of pneumonia at the age—coincidentally?—of 22. Arthur's mother has given birth to ten children, but only three remain at the time of her own death at the age of 69 in 1939. She is buried along side the body of her son, Valère, and her name is added to the headstone. Placide is left with the three children, who are by then ages 32, 37, and 39. Then in 1940, René is found dead in his Charlestown, MA apartment. He has hanged himself. Placide dies at the age of 77, with only two children who outlive him. His body is buried next to those of his wife and young son, but his name is never added to the headstone. Rosario, my grandfather, has, by then, developed some emotional problems. Married with two grown sons, he passed away at the age of 58, when I was just a toddler. Only Florida—whom I never met—lived out a natural life. She died at the age of 87 in 1989.

As one can plainly see, the loss of just one person in a family can cause so much damage; not only to the survivors, but also to the offspring of those family members. The suffering can be passed onto the proceeding generations. In his book, *A People's History of the United States* (Copyright 1980, Harper Perennial), Howard Zinn wrote of World War I, p. 359:

> *Ten million were to die on the battlefield; 20 million were to die of hunger and disease related to the war. And no one since that day has been able to show that the war brought any gain for humanity that would be worth one human life.*

Thanks & Acknowledgements

I would like to thank the following people for their invaluable contribution to this work:

Marie Rosanna Tardiff (1894-1979)
The Prioul Family
Francis Tardiff (1912-2008)
Colette LaVallée
Norman Francis LaVallée (1938-2010)
Professor Joyce Lowrie
Br. Pháp Không and the Brothers & Sisters of Blue Cliff Monastery
Barbara W. Tuchman (1912-1989)
Julia Cameron

Supporters:
Umesh Bhuju
Heather Helt Panahi
Michael O'Flynn
Alvin Hamilton
Livia Tenzer
David Greer
Patrick J. Feeley
Dr. Hugh O'Flynn
Walter Lyons
Pamela Jacobs
Tripp Mikich

Troy Pugmire
Dr. Joshua Bamberger
Jill Edelman Barberie
Lingyan Hu
Helen Greenberg
Janice Cooke
Catherine Ponte
Nora Szilagyi

In addition, I would like to thank my family—incuding my many cousins, aunts, and uncles—and most-of-all my daughter, Frannie, who have so enriched my life.

About the Author

Jeanne P. LaVallee was born in Salem, Massachusetts and brought up in Ipswich. She studied and earned degrees in French and German Literatures at Wesleyan University, the University of Cologne, and New York University. She has traveled extensively, mostly in western Europe, and has lived for periods of time in both Paris and Cologne. Since 1985, she has worked as an Educator, Writer, and Visual Artist in New England, Paris, Cologne, and New York City. She is the author of "The Impress of Heinrich Zimmer's Teachings on C.G. Jung's Profession" in the Summer, 2011 issue of *Quadrant, the Journal of the C.G. Jung Foundation for Analytical Psychology*. She now lives and works in the East Village of Manhattan with her family.